Tyrabbisaurus Rex

by A.J. Culey

Illustrated by Jeanine Henning

A.J. CULEY

TYRABBISAURUS REX

Print Edition

ISBN-13: 978-1530617098

ISBN-10: 153061709X

A POOF! Press Publication

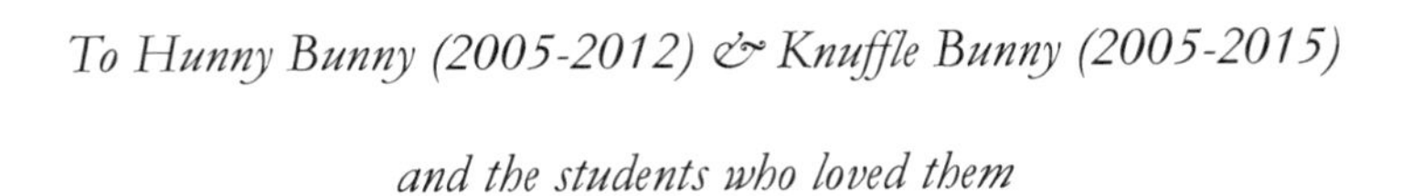
To Hunny Bunny (2005-2012) & Knuffle Bunny (2005-2015)

and the students who loved them

Tyrabbisaurus Rex

MY NAME IS Tyrabbisaurus Rex. You can call me Rex. I'm currently being held prisoner in one hideously small elementary school classroom. I do not know whether the record of these events will ever reach the outside world, but if it does, please notify the T-Rex council immediately. I expect they will be launching their rescue mission any day now. In the meantime, I will try to escape my situation without their assistance.

Also, if you happen to encounter any of those monstrously huge creatures called children, do not believe their lies. I promise that I am not, nor will I ever be, a fluffy, cuddly, lop-eared bunny rabbit. And my name is absolutely, one hundred percent, most definitely not Cuddles. What a loathsome name. I am Rex, I tell you, Rex! Not only that, but I am a Tyrabbisaurus Rex and I ROOOOAAAARRRR at you with the power of my mind.

You should bow before me and know that when I break free from this classroom, I'll wreak terror and havoc upon the human species like you've never imagined. You will bow before me or you will fall beneath my powerful claws and fearsome teeth.

And speaking of teeth, did you know that mine never stop growing? That's right. They NEVER stop growing. Which means that I can make them GROW and GROW and GROW and GROW until they have gnawed away the entire WORLD.

Oh, dear, the wardens have arrived. They think that just because they give me hay and parsley and carrot tops – ohhhhh, the carrot tops – that I will forget the torture they force me to endure day after day. Well, I will not. I will… *crunch, chomp, chomp, crunch*… not forget. Mmmmm… these carrots are especially crunchy today and such delicious leaves, *chomp, chomp, chomp*. I will have my revenge, never fear. I simply must attend to the daily chore of feeding my body so that I will be strong enough to escape this loathsome fate. Ooooh, the parsley, how utterly scrumptious, and what is this? Oh, my heavens, they brought me kale, it's like manna from the heavens, kale, mmmmmm… kale.

Chomp, chomp, I'll be right baaa – *chomp*.

Ginger

WHY DID MRS. Cavitch have to bring in a pet rabbit? Classrooms aren't supposed to have pets. I don't like that rabbit at all. Have you seen its teeth? They're huge! Plus, animals don't belong indoors with people. They're animals. They belong outside. That's what my mother said when my brothers asked for a dog, and when they asked for a turtle, and when they asked for a snake, and a ferret, and an iguana.

"Animals belong outside," she always said, and she was right. Whoever heard of a rabbit being let inside? I'd set the rabbit free, but then I'd have to get close to it. I don't care what the other kids say. Cuddle Bunny is not the right name for that rabbit. His monster teeth and the way he kicks his legs are proof of that. He should have a scary name, like the Rabbit of Death, not Cuddles. I'm not even sure he's a real rabbit. Are rabbits supposed to grow that big?

Maybe he's a mutant rabbit. Maybe someone did a bunch of experiments with animals and Cuddles is really a rabbit-dog. I guess he's kind of small for a dog, but he sure is huge for a rabbit. Every time he looks at me, I get chills. It's like his eyes are saying, "You look mighty tasty to me, human."

And why don't rabbits talk anyway? Every other animal says something. The way that rabbit acts, he should be able to roar like a lion, or at least hiss like a baby kitten, but instead all he does is thump his feet. A lot. Like we understand why he's stomping away in his house. The only time he doesn't stomp his feet is when we're feeding him, and then he's one crazy rabbit. He drags his veggies – all of them – into his house one at a time and eats them there. And when we give him his pellet food, he uses his face to shove the bowl all the way over to his house. He then darts into the house, pokes his head out to grab some food, then pulls back into the house to eat. In, out, in, out. It's like he's a turtle and the house is his shell.

Maybe that's what they mixed him with. Maybe he's a rabbit-turtle. Only not those small turtles, but those really big ones, sea turtles, the kind that could eat a baby whale. Yep, those turtles.

I just don't understand it. This is a school! People don't expect to find giant mutant rabbit-turtles chomping on hay inside a school.

Oh, great, it's Maria. That girl is ridiculous. She thinks the crazy rabbit is the cutest thing ever. Look at her, fawning all over him, and him ignoring her.

"Oh, Cuddles, aren't you the cutest thing ever?"

Blech. She's so sweet, it makes me sick.

Maria

I CANNOT BELIEVE how cute that little rabbit is. *Mi abuela* always kept *conejos* in Mexico, but they did not look like this. Plus we always ate those rabbits. I feel a little guilty, knowing that once or twice or maybe a hundred times, I ate a little guy who was just like our Cuddles. Except those rabbits were gray and not as soft. I don't think. It's not like I played with them or pet them or anything. We just kept them outside in a big hutch and when it was time to cook one, *mi abuela*

would go out to the pen and grab one and… that was that.

I love *mi abuela's* rabbit stew. Next summer, when we go visit her, she'll probably fix my favorite rabbit stew dinner, and she'll expect me to enjoy it as much as I did last summer. I wonder if I'll be able to eat it. Maybe I can pretend it's cow meat instead. Or maybe I can tell her I've decided to become a vegetarian. Except that means I can't eat any meat at all, and I don't think it'll be easy to be a vegetarian in Mexico. I'll probably starve.

Poor Cuddles. He looks so miserable inside that cage. I don't think he likes being all cooped up like that. At least he's not one of my *abuela's* bunnies about to get eaten for dinner. I'm supposed to be doing my math worksheet, but all I can think about is poor Cuddles all alone in that cage. I know we're not supposed to let him out because something bad might happen. He might get hurt or someone like my *abuela* might catch him, and then he'd get eaten after all. But he looks so lonely in there.

Maybe if I just open the cage and pet him. That sounds like a good idea. I can probably manage it without Mrs. Cavitch even noticing. The cage is so tall, it has *three* floors and *two* ramps! It's taller than me, so I can probably stand right beside it and she might not even notice. She's busy with Javon anyway.

Cuddles is on the second floor and he's staring right at me. I think he's asking me to let him out because I'm his friend. And that's what friends would do. Let him out for just a little bit of exercise. He's on the second floor though. If I leave that door open, he might get hurt trying to jump down.

Mrs. Cavitch is still talking to Javon.

I slide out of my chair and step up to the cage. I open the second floor door, just a crack, then I sneak my hand in to pet him, but he must not have noticed because he darts down the ramp toward the first floor.

I sigh and close the door again. I sit back down at my desk, but I can't stop looking at Cuddles. He's sitting on the ramp, between the first and second floors. He looks so sad.

Now Mrs. Cavitch is talking to Zing. I slip onto the floor in front of the cage and open the bottom door, just a crack. It's just enough that Cuddles can get out if he wants to. Probably he won't even notice the first floor door is open. Probably he won't even leave. Probably he'll just stay on the ramp and won't even go the rest of the way downstairs.

I think he noticed. He's heading down the ramp. Still, it's his decision. I left the door open a little, but it's really up to him, whether he wants to stay in the cage or not.

He stares at me from the bottom of the ramp and doesn't move. Maybe he won't leave if I'm too close. I scoot a little bit away. He hops forward a couple hops, but then he stops again. I lean forward and pull the cage door open a little bit further.

Cuddles barrels through the door. I manage to pet him as he streaks by. He sure is fast! And so soft.

I scoot around and watch as Cuddles hops toward Mrs. Cavitch. He stops and looks around. Then he turns and hops under Derek's chair. Derek doesn't even notice.

I slip back into my chair. My math worksheet is still waiting on my desk. I haven't done a single problem, but who can concentrate on math at a time like this?

Cuddles is free!

Cuddles pokes his head out from under Derek's chair, looks around and then darts across the aisle, stopping under Sasha's desk. She doesn't notice either.

Cuddles pops his head out, looks around and then heads for another desk.

Uh-oh. It's Ginger's. This can't be good.

Jonathan

WHEN MRS. CAVITCH told us she'd be bringing a pet to school, I thought maybe an iguana or a snake, but instead she brought that stupid, fluffy rabbit. All he ever does is sleep and eat. Mrs. Cavitch calls him Cuddle Bunny or Cuddles for short. He's kind of cute and he's definitely the softest thing I've ever touched, but come on! A snake would have been *way* cooler.

She tried to get me excited by having me feed him, but Cuddles just grabbed the parsley from my hand and ran into his house where he hunkered down with that silly bit of green leaves and glared at me as he ate. It's like he thought I might steal the parsley back or something. Honestly, I think the rabbit is kind of psycho. He may be soft, but he doesn't act like he wants anyone to cuddle him. For one thing, he stomps his feet all the time. Anytime anyone gets near his cage, he just pounds the floor like he's saying keep away.

Hey. Who let the rabbit out?

Whoa. He's headed for Ginger. Maybe I should say something. I don't think –

"Eeeeeeeek!" Ginger's shriek makes everyone jump. Even I jump and I already knew she was going to freak out when she saw him.

Ginger jumps up onto her chair and lets out another shriek. "Mrs. Cavitch, the crazy rabbit escaped! He's going to bite me! HELP!"

A snicker escapes me. Cuddles is standing right beside Ginger's desk, staring up at her. Man that rabbit really is kind of psycho. He looks like he's going to jump up there with her.

Ginger must think so too because she climbs from her chair onto the desk and wails as the rabbit follows her, jumping onto her chair and staring up at her.

"Aaaaaahhhhh! Mrs. Cavitch, he's following me! Help! Help! He's going to eat me, aaaaahhhhhh!"

Cuddles leaps for the desk, Ginger springs away and topples right off her desk, landing flat on her back.

She looks up at Cuddles, who twitches his nose at her, then jumps down and lands on top of Ginger's quivering belly.

I think for a minute Ginger might have passed out because everything is silent, then she lets out a shriek that makes me cringe.

"Eeeeeeeeeekkk!"

Mrs. Cavitch is always saying we have to be quiet because rabbits have sensitive ears, but Cuddles just blinks at her, then he turns and hops down from her belly. As soon as his feet hit the floor, he springs forward and darts right around my desk. I whip around, but he's already disappeared. Man, can that rabbit hop!

"Eeeeeeeeewwwwwww!" Ginger screams behind me. "Mrs. Cavitch, he pooped on me! HE POOPED ON ME!"

I whirl around and stare.

Ginger is right. Cuddles has pooped on her.

They're just two tiny pellets, and they're kind of hard, not runny or even really all that smelly, but you'd have thought a bird pooped on Ginger's head the way she carries on. As Ginger shrieks and wails about her dress, I laugh and laugh and laugh. I know it sounds kind of mean, but really, would you be able to hold it in? I about die, I laugh so hard.

And while I'm laughing, I can't help but think that maybe Cuddles isn't so bad after all.

Tyrabbisaurus Rex

WHAT'S WRONG WITH these humans? All I want to do is say hello to the girl dressed in pink – it's a beautiful dress and it actually looks kind of tasty. So I take a tiny, itsy-bitsy nibble out of some of her lacy frills and guess what? It *is* tasty! Anyway, I manage one tiny taste (I don't think she even noticed) and she goes nuts on me. Screaming and hollering. My ears hurt from all the noise. She makes me lose track of where I am and I kind of poop a bit. On the pink dress. That's okay though. I often poop in the same place I eat. I want to keep nibbling her dress, but then I see the teacher-warden coming. She's one huge, scary human, and she has a very scary voice. It sounds something like this:

"RAAAAAWWWWRRRRR!"

Only she actually says, "Ginger, don't move!"

I don't know who Ginger is; all I know is, it isn't me, because the name Cuddle Bunny is bad enough, but Ginger, no way am I answering to that name! So, of course, I hop away. You would think this is the signal for the start of a brand new game, the way everyone jumps up and starts hollering, which makes the teacher-warden yell even louder, only this time she says, "Everybody, freeze!"

Now I suppose I'm part of "everybody," but no teacher-warden's gonna be the boss of me. I'm a Tyrabbisaurus Rex and I decide when I'll freeze.

I hop away, this way and that, between human legs and desk legs and over chairs and under chairs and into closets and out of closets and all over that room, I hop. There's so much to see and chew. The little straps hanging down from the backpacks just call my name. So of course, I have to nibble on a few of those. Another student left out her purple gloves. I have to nibble on those too. Then I see a bright pink backpack, sitting on the floor, unzipped just a little, and inside is a nice, cozy burrow, all for me. It looks awesome.

So I climb inside and start digging around in the backpack. There are all kinds of amazing things in there – pencils and a giant, pink scarf and a bunch of papers and a book. Of course, I have to taste everything, so I start chewing. The book is the tastiest of the lot, which really is a wonderful discovery because guess what this prison has lots of? You guessed it – books. If I have to be locked up in a prison, at least there's plenty of tasty food around. After chomping a snack or three, I scrabble around, making myself a comfy nest, and curl up to take a nap.

Now you might be wondering what the humans are doing while I'm foraging, building a nest and napping. Well, the truth is, they're looking for me. I don't understand it. After all, one of me, a *thousand* of them, and not one of them sees me dart into the closet? Not one of them sees me climb into the scrumptious, pink backpack? Really weird. I think it's because humans just aren't that smart. They're certainly not smarter than me.

Anyway, I take a nap and it's a good one, at least until someone comes and snatches the backpack from the ground and wakes me up! Of course, I have to RAAAWWWRRR at them with the power of my mind. Too bad humans are too stupid to understand telepathy.

Derek

WE'VE LOOKED EVERYWHERE and we still haven't found Cuddles. It's all Ginger's fault. She scared our rabbit and now he's hiding. We'll probably never see him again. Mrs. Cavitch made sure the door stayed shut all afternoon, but still, who knows if he managed to sneak out of the classroom when we weren't looking? After all, the rabbit managed to somehow open that cage door all by himself and get free. Mrs. Cavitch says a student must have unlatched the door, but I don't think so. I think the rabbit's super-smart and he figured out how the latch works, which is really kind of amazing since some of the other kids don't know how to do that yet.

Anyway, I figure if the rabbit can get out of his cage, he probably knows how to open doors too. Now we're all lined up, ready to leave, but Mrs. Cavitch is searching everyone's backpack, just to make sure. Ginger's in front of me, with her stupid, pink dress, bouncing up and down on her toes, desperate to get home and probably wash the dress free of rabbit germs or something. She drives me crazy. She always knows the right answer to the math problems, she's always dressed like a nut (I mean, who wears a tiara to school?) and she's always, always talking about her stupid mom, who apparently knows the answers to everything, just like her daughter.

"My mom says boys are less mature than girls." Whatever that means.

"My mom says I should always look my best, even if

others don't." Please. Since when do frilly dresses and tiaras equal best-dressed?

"My mom says animals belong outside."

I glare at the back of her perfect head. Stupid, perfect Ginger, with her perfect dress and her perfect mom. She's not even worried about Cuddles and where he might be. All she cares about is her dress. She doesn't care that Cuddles could die if we don't find him. Who's going to take care of him? Who's going to feed him?

I can hear her whispering to Tanya, "It just goes to prove my mom was right."

I roll my eyes, already knowing what she's going to say next.

"Animals *do* belong outside!"

Yep. And Ginger's the one who belongs in a cage. Before I can tell her that, Mrs. Cavitch arrives to search Ginger's backpack.

"I don't think that's okay," Ginger says to Mrs. Cavitch.

Mrs. Cavitch frowns. "What's not okay, Ginger?"

"I don't think you have the right to search my backpack without a search warrant."

Mrs. Cavitch nods. "That's fine, Ginger. We won't search it then. If you get home and discover Cuddle Bunny hitched a ride, just bring him back in the morning."

"What?" Ginger screeches. "No way! He'd better not be in my backpack!" She swings the bag around, shoving it at Mrs. Cavitch. "Search it now!"

And as she shoves the backpack toward Mrs. Cavitch, Cuddle Bunny pokes his head out and twitches his nose at Ginger.

Ginger shrieks and drops the bag. Luckily, Mrs. Cavitch catches it and manages to scoop Cuddles out into her arms.

"Oh no!" Ginger wails. "I bet he pooped in my backpack too! The one my mom bought especially for me!"

She drops to her knees and looking inside, begins to wail and holler about the state of her things. She pulls out a long scarf that has several holes in it, the remains of what looks to be several pencils, and a worn-out paperback book. "My mom's *Trixie Belden* book," she whispers, tears welling in her eyes. "He chewed the corners of my mom's book."

I roll my eyes and kneel down beside her. "It's okay, Ginger. Cuddle Bunny didn't chew any of the words. Look – it's just at the corners, and now you can tell people the book is so awesome, even rabbits enjoy it!"

A tiny, watery giggle escapes Ginger's mouth.

My eyes widen in surprise. I haven't heard Ginger laugh since first grade. Back then, she was a lot of fun. She would play with us at recess and make everyone laugh at her silly jokes. Then, I don't know, something changed. She was real quiet in second grade, and she's been acting weird ever since. Now it's hard to even remember that other Ginger. Sometimes I think I made her up because the Ginger today – never running, never playing, never smiling, just talking about her mom and criticizing everyone else – that Ginger's no fun at all. She isn't easy to like or be friends with, but I've known her forever, so I guess I can stand to be nice. I help her pack everything away and when she stands up, I sling an arm around her shoulders. "I think Cuddle Bunny really likes you."

Her eyes widen. "Really?"

"Sure. Animals have a great sense of smell. He went right for you today when he escaped and then later, he hid in *your* backpack. He must like you an awful lot."

She smiles a tiny smile and ducks her head. "Still," she says quietly, "animals *do* belong outside."

I nod. "Or at the very least, in their cages."

Tyrabbisaurus Rex

FOILED AGAIN! THE mistake I made was stopping to enjoy the beautiful backpack-burrow. If I had hidden in a better spot, one that didn't remind me of a certain pink, frilly dress, the teacher-warden wouldn't have caught me at the end of the day.

She promptly puts me back in my cage and lectures me. "No more escaping, you," she says to me as she shoves me into the cage. I turn around and glare at her, but she's already latched the door and walked away.

That is one evil teacher-warden.

I storm into my house and decide to sulk for a while. Then, can you believe it? She leaves me all alone. Completely disappears. Doesn't come back for like a million years! I have to practically starve to death. All I have to eat is hay and more hay and some hay again. Sure, hay is pretty delicious, but it's not vegetables.

Plus I'm stuck.

In a cage.

And it's quiet. Spooky-quiet. No kids asking questions, no teacher talking, no pencils going scritch-scratch across paper.

Just silence.

I leave my house and head down to the second level. Nothing down here either. Just litter and hay.

I stamp a couple times just to make some noise. My claws make a skittering sound against the flooring. Yes. My fearsome claws have broken the silence.

I am Tyrabbisaurus Rex. Fear my claws of vengeance!

Oooh, hay.

I nibble a bit and wish it were a certain, tasty dress. Still yummy-good though.

It sure is dark in here, but that doesn't scare me because I'm a Tyrabbisaurus Rex. Even though I'm all alone, in the dark, with no one around, I –

What are you looking at?

The giant, stuffed tiger across the room is staring at me. I know he is. I can't see him, but I know he's out there, looking at me with those beady eyes.

Next time I get out, I'm going to bite that tiger's nose off.

Stop staring at me, I mind-roar at him, but he doesn't answer. Does no one use their brains for communication anymore?

I race back up the ramp and storm into my house where I hunker down, bored and mad.

Stupid tiger.

Why does he get to be outside the cage, but I'm stuck in here?

Evil humans and their evil plans to lock up fierce Tyrabbisaurus Rexes.

Ginger

TODAY I'M GOING to wear the white skirt with purple flowers that my mom made for me. It has a matching blouse and when I wear the two together, I remember having tea with her. We'd both dress in our skirts and blouses, mine with the purple flowers and hers with the blue ones, and we'd wear our matching hats. We'd drink our tea and eat cookies and talk about girl stuff.

I get dressed, already planning how I'm going to tell everyone at school about teatime with my mom. I put on my hat and stare at myself in the mirror. I can almost hear my mom telling me how beautiful I look. I'm about to leave my room when I remember Cuddles, the poopy rabbit.

What if he ruins this outfit too?

I sigh and change my clothes.

Stupid rabbit.

*

I grumble all the way to the bus stop. I'm still wearing my hat because no rabbit's going to stop me from looking my best, but it's just not right to wear such a fancy hat with jeans.

When the bus arrives, I climb on, still grumbling. The other kids at the bus stop give me weird looks, but I don't care. They didn't get pooped on by a rabbit, did they? I bet they'd be grumbling too if that evil bunny targeted them.

I throw myself into a seat and cross my arms. Stupid rabbit.

"Hi!" Maria pops up from the seat in front of me and gives me a huge smile.

I roll my eyes and ignore her. Maybe she'll go away.

"I love your hat," she gushes.

I don't want to talk, but I can't be rude when she's complimenting my hat, now can I? "Thank you," I say. "My mother –"

"I bet Cuddles would like it. He's the cutest bunny ever and he really likes you. I bet he'd like you even more if you showed him your hat."

Seriously? I give her an incredulous look. "You know he pooped on me, don't you?"

"Well, it was only a couple little balls and they didn't smell or anything. I'm sure he feels bad."

Is this girl for real? That rabbit isn't sorry and if I let

him touch my hat, he'd ruin it too. I tell her just that, then I add, "He's a devil-bunny!"

Maria gasps. "He is not. He's sweet and precious and adorable."

Someone snorts from across the aisle. It's Jonathan.

"What's that supposed to mean?" Maria demands.

"It means Ginger's right. That bunny's full of the devil. My gran says that about me, so I think I'd notice it in a rabbit, and believe me, the devil's there all right."

I giggle, but Maria's face is getting red.

"That's not true," she shouts at Jonathan. "That bunny is sweet and he loves us."

"Are you serious? The bunny can't stand us," I say. "He stamps his feet at us all the time."

"That's true," Derek leans around Jonathan to say. "He's no Cuddle Bunny, no matter his name."

Maria lets out a huff, turns around and plops down on her seat. She refuses to speak to us for the rest of the ride, a lovely turn of events if you ask me.

Tyrabbisaurus Rex

FINALLY, AFTER ABOUT ten trillion hours of darkness, the room gets bright again and the teacher-warden comes back.

I can't believe she left me all alone like that. I yell at her with the power of my mind, but she just hurries around the room, doing other things, completely ignoring me.

Why aren't you listening to me, I roar at her, but of course, she doesn't reply to a single thought. *How could you leave me alone like that?* I shout at her.

Nothing.

You know I'm right and that's why you're ignoring me, isn't it? I stamp my feet at her, but she doesn't even notice. I stamp my feet again.

She finally looks at me, so I shout, *How could you leave me alone like that?*

"Are you hungry, baby-poo?"

Hungry? Of course, I'm hungry. I'm a Tyrabbisaurus Rex, aren't I? But that's not the point, I tell her. *You left me all alone for a billion years!*

You'll never believe what she does next. Does she apologize? Does she promise to never leave me alone again? Does she let me out of my prison?

No, she does not!

Because she is the queen of evil, the duchess of darkness, the wickedest warden in all the land, she does something terrible.

She gives me vegetables.

And not just any vegetables. We're not talking lettuce here, people. We're talking… kale. And cabbage! She gives me cabbage.

I heard some of the kids calling her Mrs. Cabbage. I wonder if she has her very own cabbage patch. I wonder if she'll let me visit sometime. I wonder…

But it's wrong, so wrong. She's trying to make me enjoy my captivity. Well, I won't. It's not right, I tell you. When a monstrous T-Rex falls in love with his provider of vegetables, that's okay… as long as the provider doesn't keep him captive. But she does. She locks me away and expects me to –

These veggies are so delicious.

She expects me to –

I've never had this veggie before. I wonder what it is. Giant, green leaves, has to be completely awesome. I take a huge bite.

Ack, ack, ack!

What is that? Disgusting, disgusting, disgusting, drag it away and stomp it deep into the litter, deep, deep, deep.

So that's her plan. To beguile me with yummy veggies, only to sneak in a vile, disgusting impostor-vegetable that no self-respecting Tyrabbisaurus Rex would ever eat. She's trying to poison me!

I wonder if that means I shouldn't eat the rest of the vegetables. I pick through them carefully. They look and smell so delicious.

I glare at the green disgustingness peeking out at me from the litter box. I storm over and kick some more litter on top of it. Stupid green thing masquerading as a vegetable. That is so wrong.

"Bunny-boooooo."

She's back. And she's talking out loud again. Why can't she communicate telepathically? Are all humans this stupid? Is this why none of them talk to me with the power of their minds? Because they have to actually speak out loud?

That's just so wrong.

"What's the matter, sweetie-pie?" she croons to me in a singsong voice. "Cuddly Bunny, baby-poo, what's the matter, sweetums?"

Why is she talking like that? Like I can't understand what she's saying. She's talking to me like I'm a baby or something. Any minute now, she's going to start ootchie-gootchie-gooing.

"Cuddle Bunny," she croons that loathsome name again.

Why doesn't anyone understand? My name is Rex. Tyrabbisaurus Rex.

"Didn't you like the mustard greens, bunnykins?"

Mustard greens? Is that the name of those disgusting vegetable impostors? Of course, I don't like them! They aren't even vegetables. I know my vegetables. And no vegetable could possibly taste so disgusting.

"Here you go, baby. I've got you a little treat." She holds out in her hand something that smells so divine, I can't help myself. I lean forward and snatch up the treat.

Hunkering over my special treat, I gobble it down – delicious, smooth yumminess – so delicious I almost forget to guard my bowl against more impostor-veggies.

"I guess you like yogurt chips, don't you?"

I don't know what a yogurt chip is, but I'm pretty sure it's some fancy name for VEGETABLE. Yes! I love vegetables. But, just so we're clear, I do NOT love the provider of said vegetables. She's still evil. Evil. Evil. Evil.

*

The girl who wore the pink lace dress yesterday comes to school wearing jeans and a t-shirt today. I'd be a little disappointed – those jeans look too tough for chewing – except her head looks divine. It's covered in purple flowers!

Yesterday, pink was my favorite color, but today it's definitely purple. And the girl with the tasty dress is definitely my favorite human, even though she does have a screechy voice.

I stare at her head for hours, imagining the possibilities. I already have my route planned. All I need is a running start. I'll race under those two desks, then around that desk there, then I'll jump on that chair, hop from it to the table and from there I'll leap for her head. It's going to be awesome.

I'll turn the scarf-thing into shredding for my nest and I'll eat the flowers. I don't know what I'll do with the hat. It's kind of big for a nest. A lot big.

The human called Jonathan can't even see around her it's that big.

I could try to eat the hat. You never know – it could be delicious.

Jonathan

GIRLS ARE SO weird.

Ginger comes to school today dressed like normal for once, except her head looks like a purple garden exploded all over it. She has on this big, straw hat that's almost too big to fit in the classroom door. It has a purple scarf-thing tied around it in a gigantic bow and there are flowers everywhere, like a flower shop vomited purple all over her head. It's really weird. When she sits down at her desk, I can't see the board because her flower-head is so big!

Even though I think Ginger's weird, I actually kind of like the hat once I realize that Mrs. Cavitch can't see me sitting behind it. I hide behind Flower-Head and tear all the erasers out of my pencils. I then break them up into tiny pieces and start firing them around the room.

Pow pow pow! Three to the back of Maria's head. Sweet!

Maria grabs her hair and looks around. I duck behind Flower-Head and wait a moment before peeking out again. All clear.

Pow pow pow pow! Four to the T-Rex poster, right on his giant dinosaur nose. Awesome!

Pow-pow-pow, pow-pow-pow! Six to the back of Derek's head, lightning fast.

Derek swivels around, but I hide behind Flower-Head again.

Woohoo! This is so awesome, I can't even believe it. Maybe Ginger would be willing to wear a hat every day. Who knew that having such a strange-looking head could be so awesomely cool?

Pow-pow-pow-pow-pow! Five to the blackboard where Mrs. Cavitch is writing an assignment. Uh-oh.

I duck behind Flower-Head again and quickly scoop my ammunition into the palm of my hand. Hiding the evidence in the pocket of my jeans, I smile innocently at Mrs. Cavitch as she walks past Flower-Head to stand by my desk.

"Jonathan," Mrs. Cavitch speaks quietly. "What are you up to back here?"

I shake my head. "Nothing, Mrs. Cavitch."

"I see." She looks at my empty desk. "Well, Jonathan, you're not supposed to be doing nothing. You're supposed to be working on the math assignment on the board."

"But, Mrs. Cavitch," I protest innocently. "I can't see the board from here. Flower-Head, I mean, Ginger's hat is in the way."

"Hmmm." She stares at me with that stern teacher look. Every teacher I've ever had uses the Look. They stare at you like they can see right into your brain, straight to every bad thought you ever had, and you just can't help but squirm. You know that one more second of that scary gaze and you'll admit everything you've done wrong since the day you entered kindergarten.

I can feel all those confessions – the day I stuffed paper towels down the kindergarten toilets just to see what would happen (the toilets overflowed and we got an extra-long recess while the floors were mopped), the day I tied Suzie's long hair to Karla's during a movie in first grade (who knew two girls could scream so loudly?), the day I accidentally on purpose dialed 911 from the classroom phone in second grade (the police came and everything – it was so cool!), the many eraser fire-balls I had launched in every classroom I'd ever been in – all of these confessions are bubbling to the surface when Mrs. Cavitch turns to Flower-Head and says quietly, "Ginger, please put your hat in the closet, and Jonathan –" She gives me The Look again, then in a very serious, scary voice, growls, "Get to work. Now!"

"Yes, ma'am," we both murmur.

Ginger gets up and heads for the closet while I quickly pull out my math notebook. As I work, I congratulate myself on my legendary successes that day. I had launched *eighteen* eraser fire-balls that morning with zero consequences!

This is my best record yet and I owe it all to Flower-Head. Girls are still weird, but this is one example of their weirdness that I can actually enjoy. Oh, yeah!

Maria

I LOVE GINGER's hat. It is so beautiful. And just like I told her, Cuddles likes it too. He keeps staring at it. I bet he would like to play with the hat, or maybe sleep in it. Mrs. Cavitch said she's going to let Cuddles out to play during recess.

I wonder if he'll crawl into my backpack like he did Ginger's. I think I'll leave my backpack on the floor. I'll leave it open so he'll know he can go inside and sleep. I wish he had slept in my backpack the other day. I would have been so excited if Mrs. Cavitch had told me I could take the backpack home, even though Cuddles might be inside it. I would love the chance to take him home. I don't know why Ginger freaked out. That rabbit is the cutest bunny ever!

I think I'll make sure there are plenty of things on the floor for Cuddles to play with during recess. Since we won't be in here to play with him, he might get bored.

"Line up for recess, class," Mrs. Cavitch calls.

I quickly run into the closet and set my backpack on the floor. I unzip it and try to make it look inviting so Cuddles will enjoy it. As I stand up, I notice Ginger's hat sitting on the shelf above the hooks holding our backpacks and jackets. I bet Cuddles would love my backpack if it was sitting next to Ginger's hat. I grab her hat and carefully set it beside my backpack. No, that won't work. Cuddles might just go to the hat and ignore my backpack. I have to make my backpack more exciting than the hat.

I turn Ginger's hat upside down and stuffed some of the flowers and the bow trailing from the hat into my backpack. I peel back the top of the backpack so the purple flowers and bow are visible and nod my head. It's perfect. Jumping up, I run from the closet and dart out of the classroom into the hallway. The class is heading around the corner. I race toward them and catch up just as they reach the outside door. Mrs. Cavitch holds the door open for us and as we head outside, she says, "Have a nice recess!"

As the door closes behind me, I notice the kindergarten teachers are on the playground. I love it when they have recess duty. They always play with us and make recess a lot more fun. I love this part of the day!

Mrs. Cavitch

"WELL, MY DARLING Cuddly-wuddly, it's just you and me for recess time. You want to get out and run and play? Come here, sweetums." I open the cage and try to coax Cuddle Bunny out of his house, but he just glowers at me. Doesn't he know I'm about to give him his freedom? Why is everything so difficult? Sighing, I reach in and gently tip his house over and pull it away, revealing a very angry Cuddle Bunny. He stamps his feet at me and hurtles down his ramp. Shaking my head, I go to the second level, but as I open that cage door, he races down to the first level. Well, that works.

I reach down and open the first level's cage door, step back and wait. Cuddles just stares at the door and doesn't move. I don't think he trusts me yet. Maybe this isn't such a good idea. What if I can't catch him at the end of recess? The kids only have twenty minutes for recess and five minutes have already passed. I really don't know how much time it will take me to catch him once I've let him out. It could be forever. Maybe I should just –

Too late. Cuddles explodes out of the cage and tears across the classroom. I turn to watch. Really, the rabbit is too cute for words. Already he is leaping and twisting and turning, tearing from one side of the room to the other, sniffing everything, jumping up and down and scoping all around. This was definitely a good idea. I haven't seen Cuddles so active since I got him. He seems to vibrate with joy, he is so thrilled to be out and running.

Settling at my desk, I lean back in my chair and take pictures of Cuddle Bunny running and playing. Recess. I truly love this part of the day.

Ginger

A LOT OF kids begin a game of kickball while others head for the jungle gym. I watch for a few minutes before turning toward the swings. I'm almost to them when I remember. I'm wearing jeans today. For once I don't have to worry about ruining my outfit.

I can play kickball or climb the jungle gym or play

tag. I can do anything today, maybe even jump rope with the kindergarten teachers.

The teachers are turning the ropes for Maria and her little brother who race in to jump together. They're both laughing.

It looks like a lot of fun.

I look down at my jeans and back toward Maria. She and her brother race out from under the spinning ropes and two kindergartners dart in.

"Hey, Ginger! Come play kickball!" Derek hollers, beckoning to me from where he's playing.

Maybe I'll do both.

"In a minute," I call back.

I run over to where Maria's playing with her brother. "Can I jump?" I ask.

"Sure," Maria says. "Let's go in together!" She grabs my hand and we run into the swinging ropes.

As we jump, Maria chants a jump rope song, only instead of singing 'Teddy Bear, Teddy Bear,' she's saying 'Bunny Bear, Bunny Bear.'

It doesn't even make sense – what kind of bunny is a bear – but I'm too busy trying to turn around and touch the ground while jumping rope to protest and then we get tangled in the rope and have to stop.

We giggle and giggle, then get back in line to try again.

Even though the song is silly and doesn't make any sense at all, the next time we jump, I sing along as we pretend to climb stairs and slap our shoes.

"Bunny Bear, Bunny Bear, take a bow..."

After we jump a third time and miss when trying to do the splits, I leave Maria jumping with her brother so I can join the kickball game.

It's the best recess ever.

Tyrabbisaurus Rex

I DON'T KNOW what just happened. I'm pretty sure it's a trap, but I'm not going to let that stop me. Freedom is calling again and I love it. I race around the room, sniffing everything I see. The teacher-warden is staring at me. She must be planning something terrible. That's okay. I'm planning something too. My big escape!

I race to the center of the classroom, then stand up on my hind legs and scope around. There are about a million desks in this room and maybe twenty million books. The only thing I don't see is a door. There has to be one though because the monster-children aren't in here anymore. I think they're hiding it from me.

Time to explore. I have a door to find.

I head out into enemy territory, aware that danger is all around me. I find a piece of paper on the floor. I take a couple bites. Delicious!

I dart under the computer table. The table is very strange. It has a lot of tails, some thin and short and others thick and so long they disappear into the wall. I chew a couple of the thin ones, but they aren't very tasty.

I turn around and from under the table, stare out at the rest of the room. On the wall across from me is a huge picture of me. It's a pretty cool picture. I'm standing on my hind legs and I'm roaring at people with the power of my mind. My claws are totally fearsome and my teeth look sharp enough to snap a person in half. My name is written across the giant picture in huge letters. Tyrabbisaurus Rex. I'm so famous, it's awesome.

I hop forward to stand in front of the picture, admiring how ferocious I look. I bet if I stood like that for the children, they wouldn't call me Cuddles anymore. I practice standing tall, my claws in front of me, teeth ready for chewing. Yep. I am FIERCE!

I decide to run some more. I race across the room and find a book sitting on the floor. It's a book about animals. It has a picture of a bat on the cover. Why anyone would want to read about bats, I don't know. They eat bugs. I decide to chew the corner of the book, just a little. Delicious. I nibble on one of the bat's wings, then take off running. Yes! This is the best place ever.

I race around the classroom twice. The second time, I leap forward, twist my body mid-air and race back the other way. I'm really good at this running thing. No one can catch me. I'm super-fast!

After testing my reflexes for about ten hours, I decide it's time to take a nap. I find myself a nice, cozy place along the wall, in between two bookshelves and I fall asleep.

This is the life.

Hey! What's happening?

The evil teacher-warden just scooped me up and put me back in my cage. I can't believe I forgot to escape while I was free. I can't believe I let her find me. I was hidden in the perfect spot and she still found me. She is so evil.

Now I'm back in the cage. But good news because now I know where the door is. I was glaring at the teacher-warden, roaring at her with the power of my mind, telling her how evil she is (she's still too stupid to understand, no surprise there) when she suddenly opened the door and disappeared through it.

Ha! Now I know where to go the next time I'm out of the cage. Freedom here I come!

Maria

AS SOON AS we get back to the classroom, I race to the closet to check my backpack. It's lying exactly where I left it.

I peek inside, but Cuddle Bunny isn't hiding there.

Ginger's hat is still sitting on the ground next to my backpack, but I don't think Cuddles even took a nibble.

I examine both closely and can't find any evidence that he curled up on either of our things.

I am so disappointed!

Shaking my head, I place Ginger's hat back on the rack, hang up my backpack and leave the closet.

Derek

WE SPEND THE afternoon in writers workshop. Mrs. Cavitch gives us a writing prompt. I'm supposed to write about someone important in my life. I keep thinking about recess and how Ginger joined our kickball game. I'd forgotten what a good kicker she is.

I was thinking about writing about Cuddle Bunny,

but I don't have a lot to say about him. I could write about my mom, but I always write about her. Why do teachers give us the same writing prompts year after year? Don't they know we get tired of writing the same thing over and over again?

I think maybe I'll write about my friends, but I've written about them before too. So I decide to write about Ginger because I don't know who else to write about and I actually have a lot to say about her.

I write about how she used to tell funny jokes in kindergarten – knock-knock jokes and silly puns. I write about how she used to make up tongue-twisters in first grade and how she'd be the first to try them and would always make us laugh because she sounded so funny saying them. I write about how she got real quiet in second grade and one day just stopped telling jokes and how she hasn't really laughed or played since.

I write about how she wore jeans for the first time today and how I think it's Cuddle Bunny's fault. I write that I'm happy Cuddle Bunny pooped on her dress because today Ginger came to school in jeans and because she wore jeans, she played kickball with me.

I write about my friend Ginger and how Cuddle

Bunny gave her back to me.

Then I decide Cuddle Bunny deserves a reward.

I wait until the end of the day when everyone's getting ready to go home and I sneak him a treat. Mrs. Cavitch keeps a bag of yogurt chips on her desk and I know Cuddle Bunny loves them.

I settle on the floor in front of the cage, then open the door a crack.

I hold out my hand and Cuddle Bunny gobbles up the chips real fast.

"Derek, what are you doing? It's time to go!" Mrs. Cavitch calls from the doorway.

"I'm coming." I jump up, set the bag of yogurt chips on a desk and grab my backpack. "Bye, Cuddle Bunny," I call over my shoulder as I race out the door.

*

Ginger's sitting by herself on the bus again.

I plop down beside her. "How's it going?"

"Okay," she says.

Silence.

Jeez. She never talks anymore.

"I hope you wear jeans again tomorrow," I blurt out.

She looks surprised. "Why?" she asks. "They're so ugly."

"They're just jeans. They're not supposed to be fancy."

"My dresses are fancy," she says.

"But you can't run in your dresses."

"So?"

"So I liked playing with you today. You don't play when you wear your dresses."

"I know."

"You can bring a hat every day or a fancy scarf. That way –"

"My hat! Oh, no," Ginger moans.

"What's wrong?"

"I left my hat at school. Oh, what if the rabbit gets it? What if he ruins it like he ruined my dress?"

I roll my eyes. "The rabbit's in his cage. He's not gonna get your hat."

"But what if he does? My mom gave me that hat, Derek. It's important to me."

"Okay, calm down. We'll go straight to the classroom in the morning, okay? Right after we get off the bus, we'll go see Mrs. Cavitch."

"Before breakfast?"

"Before everything."

"Okay. Thanks, Derek."

"You're welcome. So. Tomorrow –"

Ginger smiles. "I'll wear my jeans. I won't even bring a fancy hat because I already have one at school." She stands up. "This is my stop." She climbs over me and heads down the aisle. When she reaches the door, she glances back and says, "Thanks, Derek," and disappears down the stairs.

I smile all the way home.

Tyrabbisaurus Rex

THE HUMANS ARE gone again. Why do they keep leaving me all alone like this?

Oh, good. Mrs. Cabbage is back. I'm not happy because I like her or anything. I just hope she has some veggies for me.

She does. Oh, happy days. I race up the ramp to the second floor and then around and up to the third floor where she's filling my bowl with delicious, scrumptious, wondrous-smelling veggies. I sniff them carefully – have to be sure there are no impostor veggies lurking around. Nope. No impostors there. I grab a hunk of parsley and dart into my house.

Yum. This parsley is incredible.

I finish it, race out to grab a cabbage leaf, then race back into the house. I do this for a long while. These veggies are absolutely wonderful. Every last one of them.

I'm very sad when the bowl is empty. It's just the saddest thing ever because I know what it means. No more veggies until tomorrow.

Mrs. Cabbage is ready to leave me. I can tell because she has her purse and bag and she's heading for the door with her keys in hand.

"Bye, sweetums," she calls to me as she closes the door behind her.

It's so quiet. Again. I head down the ramp and stare out into the classroom. There's that stupid tiger again, staring at me.

Stop staring at me, I roar at it. *In fact, do something useful. Come over here and open this cage.*

Nothing. That tiger is worthless.

I head down the second ramp to the bottom floor. I plop down on the floor and stare at the door. It's just not right that I'm imprisoned while that tiger roams free. Is that door latched? I tilt my head to get a better view.

I don't think it's latched.

I stand up and hop over to the door. I nudge it with my nose and it swings open. Oh, that wonderful little human who gave me the yummy yogurt treats. He must have forgotten to latch the door. I just love those kids.

I hop down into the land of the free. Yes!

Where to first? So many possibilities, but I know exactly where to begin. I'm about to start on my journey when I smell something. Something amazing. Something that smells like vegetable yogurt goodness.

I sniff my way around a desk. The smell is right here. Right here. Right –

Above me.

I look up. Ha! I jump up on the chair and stand on my hind legs. I swipe at that beautiful bag and it falls to the floor. I pounce on it.

For about a hundred hours, I wrestle with that bag. It's determined to keep those yogurt chips from me, but I will prevail.

Finally, finally, after much nibbling and chewing and shaking of the bag, it pops open and it's a yogurt chip party! I eat and eat and wrestle with the bag until I suddenly remember – I have another mission, but I can't leave my yogurt chips behind. Oh no.

And so I drag them with me.

I follow the exact same route I planned out earlier in the day when I was hoping to snag me a purple hat. Only this time I have different prey in mind.

I race under two desks, then around another one.

There's a bookshelf near, so I stash my treasure there. I'll come back for it later. I get back on route.

I jump onto a chair, then hop from it to the table. I race across the table and take a giant leap for the counter that runs along the side of the room.

Like I said, all I need is a running start.

I race down the counter and leap for the tiger's head.

Veggie-awesomeness!

The tiger tumbles to the floor and I jump after it.

I land right on its nose. Hyaw!

I settle my hind feet into its belly. I scratch at its face, then I nibble on its cheek.

The tiger doesn't fight back.

That's completely uncool.

You're so boring, I tell the tiger.

He just stares at me with his blank eyes.

I tilt my head so I can look into them better.

Nothing but stupidity stares back.

Yep. This tiger is definitely the dumbest of the bunch.

I nibble on his nose.

He might be dumb, but he sure is tasty.

I hop off his belly and attack his tail. It's so long and cool. I chomp down hard on its tip, but that tiger doesn't even flinch.

I race around the tiger and sink my teeth into his ear. I work on dragging him toward my cage. I want him in there. That's my goal. I keep pulling, but man, that tiger is heavy.

I have a plan though. Can't give up. I have a plan.

I'm going to drag the tiger to the cage and stuff him inside it. It'll be awesome. Tiger locked in the cage, Tyrabbisaurus Rex free on the outside. Then I'll be the one staring at him, laughing at his captivity.

I keep tugging, but after a thousand hours of pulling, I only manage to pull that giant tiger an inch.

Or maybe a centimeter. I'm telling you, that tiger is abnormally large.

Tigers should not outweigh fierce Tyrabbisaurus Rexes!

I finally collapse. I curl up beside the tiger and take a little nap.

*

I wake a while later and decide I need some food if I'm going to be moving giant, stubborn tigers. The question is – what shall I eat? I could go for some hay (yummy deliciousness), but the cage is so far away from my goal: the door. It's still all the way over on the other side of the room and there are so many other things I could chew along the way to freedom.

Suddenly I remember my treasure. Now where did I stash that thing? I sniff my way around the tiger, no yogurt chips there, but I decide to do some taste-testing. After all, there may be something even better than yogurt chips to eat around here (although I find that hard to believe).

I nibble on the tiger's side a little – still tasty – then hop away.

I'm close to the closet where I found the backpack-burrow the other day. Maybe there'll be something yummy to eat in there. On the way, I find my yogurt chips – hurray! They're right where I left them – on the bookshelf next to a book about cars. I drag the bag out, shake it until two yogurt chips fall out. I eat them, then I pounce on the bag. I stamp all over it, but sadness. There's nothing left inside. I ate all the yogurt chips, all of them!

Unless –

I turn and stare back at the tiger. *Did you eat my yogurt chips?* I yell at him.

No answer.

I race back to the tiger. *Those were mine I was saving for later. They are not tiger food.* I jump onto his belly, hop toward his head and stare down into his face. *Bad tiger,* I tell him, but he doesn't answer.

I lean over and chew on his mouth. Yep, still tasty.

I remember my mission to explore the closet. I jump down and hop toward it.

I'm still hungry so on the way, I eat a piece of paper, nibble on two paperback books (well they left them on the floor – what do they expect?) and chew a hole in the carpet. Hey, it was there and I was walking on it and I suddenly wondered – what does that taste like? Maybe it'll be yummy. Truthfully, it was kind of disgusting, but I didn't stop until I had a perfectly round hole. Otherwise, the carpet would look uneven and wrong.

The closet is mostly empty. All the lovely backpack-burrows have gone home with the children. So sad. There's something on the ground though, something that has definite possibilities. It's a human-sized sweatshirt.

You know the best thing about human clothing? It has holes. Holes that are perfect for me. They're Tyrabbisaurus Rex-sized. I crawl in the neck hole, then make a turn and crawl down a long arm-tunnel. I find the end of the tunnel, poke my head through and start chewing. This blue stuff is really kind of tasty. Not quite as tasty as the pink dress from yesterday, or even as good as the paper I ate earlier today, but pretty yummy all the same. After a few nibbles, I push my way out of the tunnel and turning around, notice the sweatshirt has a giant picture on it.

I tilt my head, trying to see what the picture is. I think it's… it's… argh!

It's a dog! Who would put a picture of a dog in the middle of my sweatshirt-nest? Don't these people know that dogs like to chase Tyrabbisaurus Rexes and sometimes even eat them? That's just not right. I stamp my feet all over that dog's face, but that doesn't really do any good. He just grins up at me like he knows I'll be awfully tasty and he's planning to eat my brains. Well, I won't let him.

I pace around the blue sweatshirt-nest and make my

plans. I'll stamp on him again. I race over and pound my feet all over that puppy's ears, but it doesn't work. He doesn't even yelp or cry at all. I pace some more and think. I know. I'll eat that puppy's face! This is a great plan. I'll eat his face so he can't stare at me, plus I am kind of hungry.

It'll be like a special treat for me. A puppy treat!

And so I eat the puppy's face. It's really tasty. But then the puppy's paws look kind of lonesome, so I eat those too. Then I use my claws to scratch up his body and drag all the scraps into the neck-tunnel and make myself a nest. Then I curl up in the middle of my doggy-scraps and take a little nap.

I make the best nests! I truly am the king of nest-makers. The emperor of nests. The superhero of the mighty T-Rexes. The hero of every.... Zzzzzzz...

*

I open one eye. Scraps of puppy surround me. He was yummy, but now I'm hungry again and I want more than just puppy scraps. I want veggies.

I stand up and stretch out my legs. I twitch my ears and hop to the door of the closet. I stare out into the darkened classroom. No one's in here. I stare across the room toward where I think the door is. It's so far away, I can't even see it. There are a thousand desks between me and it, but that's okay. I'm on a mission.

I hop forward and then I dart under a desk. I stand there a few minutes, then dart forward again, around one desk, under another desk, stop beneath a third. I creep out from under that desk, stand up on my hind legs and scope around. No one's near me, just more desks. Why are there so many desks in this crazy place?

I run around three more desks and then I run around them again. Fun. I stop and look around. I run around all three of the desks again. Just because I can. Because no one's here and this is fun.

I run across the next aisle, under one more desk and come out in front of the door. The door! I made it to the door. I can't believe it. I dart forward and stare up. It's really big.

I see the handle. I need to pull it down to get the door open. No problem. I'm a Tyrabbisaurus Rex and I can jump higher than – ooh, more books.

I dart over to nibble on a couple books. They're just so yummy.

As I nibble on my book, I stare at the doorknob. I can do this. I can totally do this. Running start. Leap forward and – nothing. I'm an amazing jumper, but the handle's just too high.

This is going to take some time. I look around.

Chair. I hop on it.

Table. I hop on the table.

Oooh. More funny tails, this time from a keyboard and a –

Mouse!

I pounce. The mouse slides a bit, but doesn't fight back.

I nibble on its tail. Can you believe the mouse doesn't even move? If someone chewed on my tail, I'd bite their nose off.

I pounce on the keyboard's tail and nibble it too. Hey, I need the energy. For my grand escape.

I stare at the handle. It's not so far now. All I have to do is leap just right and the door will open and freedom, here I come.

Laughter.

I can't believe it. Are the humans coming back already?

I hear the jingle of something and the handle starts to wiggle. This is going to be awesome. I twitch my whiskers as I prepare for my great escape.

The handle turns slowly, the door begins to open and I leap for freedom.

I skid past the door so fast, all I see are a blur of human shoes and then I'm off.

This is super-awesome. There's a ginormous track in front of me. It goes on and on and on. I hear the humans shouting behind me and one of them is wailing, "Oh, no, Cuddle Bunny," but nothing can stop me now. I'm super-saurus!

There are other humans up ahead. They don't see me yet. They're just standing around talking. They're huge.

I zip around one shoe that has triangular heels about as tall as me on the bottom of it. Don't ask me why. Humans are weird.

The owner of those shoes shrieks in alarm as I dart around a corner.

I race down another long corridor. The floor is mighty slippery out here. Kind of fun actually.

I see an open door and I barrel through it. I dart under a cart and hide there listening.

"Where'd he go?" someone asks. I think it's Mrs. Cabbage.

"What was that?" The voice is shrill and hurts my ears. I bet it's the woman with the giant shoes. "Was that a rat? I won't work in a school with rats."

A rat! I'm a fierce Tyrabbisaurus Rex. I don't have a rat tail. I have a giant Rex-sized tail.

I twitch my nose. That woman's rude, insulting my tail like that.

"He's our classroom rabbit," Mrs. Cabbage wails. "What are we going to do? The kids will be here any minute. They'll be so sad if something happens to poor Cuddle Bunny."

I don't believe her at all. She's trying to trick me, make me feel guilty for running away. Well, I don't feel guilty. Not at all. They should feel guilty for locking me up like a criminal.

I look around the room. You'll never believe where I am.

Outside's probably what you're thinking, right? Well, wrong!

Here I planned my big escape and all I did was escape into another stupid classroom. It has lots and lots of tables instead of desks, but still. It's basically the same.

I move around, sniffing at everything. I'm terribly hungry and I doubt this classroom has any vegetables at all. If only I'd escaped outside. I could have eaten grass and dandelions. I'm sure that would have been a delicious breakfast.

Suddenly I smell something.

It smells really good. Like super-awesome good. I sniff my way all around the room, but the smell isn't in this room. It's out there.

I look at the door. It's still cracked a bit, just like it was when I entered this room. I hop toward it.

Seriously. That smell is divine. It's calling my name, it's so strong.

Tyrabbisaurus Rex, it whispers.

Or maybe it said Cuddle Bunny. I'm not sure. I can't concentrate because that is the best smell ever.

I'm at the door and I poke my nose out. I look around. The ginormous humans are all gone. But there, right in the middle of the floor is something green. I dart toward it and gobble it up. It has all these tiny little leaves on it and they taste scrumptious.

I mean wow. Wow. Wow. Wow.

I don't know what this is, but it's just wow.

There's another one.

I hop toward that piece and I gobble it up too. I've never tasted anything like it. It's not kale or parsley. It's not hay. I love those things, but this is incredible. It's so strong, so spicy, so vegetabley good.

I see another one. It's a little further down the hall. I stand there and stare at the yummy goodness, listening close. I don't hear any tall humans talking or walking or breathing funny. I mean, you've noticed that, haven't you? The way they breathe? It's so loud.

Anyway, I don't hear them and better yet, I don't smell them. Maybe because all I smell is yummy vegetable goodness.

I dart forward and snatch it up. A giant shadow falls over me and I freeze. Huge hands are reaching for me. No way, buster.

I dart away, between a couple legs down the hallway, around a corner and kaboom. I slide right into another pair of legs. I jump up, but before I can take off again, someone scoops me up. How rude.

This person knows how to hold a Tyrabbisaurus Rex just right. She's got one hand right under my tail, supporting my back legs and another hand under my belly and she's got me against her chest, right under her chin. Feels kind of good, but that's not right.

"I gotcha, little Cuddly Bunny-Boo."

What? No way. Mrs. Cabbage is the one who's holding me just right. *Put me down, Mrs. Cabbage*, I yell at her in my mind, but she still hasn't figured out how to communicate with me. What is this woman's problem?

She's walking back, all the long way that I ran.

But I ran so far. I ran and got so far away and now she's taking me back to where I started from. That's just not right. I want to stamp my feet at her, but she's holding them. I want to kick, but I can't. Why is she such a good Tyrabbisaurus Rex holder?

Suddenly we're at the classroom door. The same one I escaped from a thousand years ago. She opens it and walks me back across the room to – you guessed it – the cage.

"There you go, my sweetie-pie," she croons as she sets me down inside the cage. "Back in your condo you go. I can't imagine how you got free."

I glower at her, then turn and storm into my house. I stomp my feet a few times, but she just laughs. What's wrong with her? Why is she laughing when I'm so mad?

I stamp again to show her that this is an unacceptable response, but do you know what she says to me? She says, "That is just so cute."

Ugh.

What am I supposed to do with these crazy humans? They can't communicate with me. They don't even understand the simplest of Tyrabbisaurus protocols

(how can she think I'm stamping my feet for her amusement?)

"Here you go, sweetie," she interrupts me and puts those wonderful tiny leafy things in front of my nose. "Have some cilantro." I immediately start chomping away at this cilantro-vegetable that I've never heard of before, but that I love, love, love.

Humans sure are annoying, but they make the most incredible vegetables ever. I may forgive her. Just this once.

Derek

THIS DAY IS crazy-weird. And that bunny is a bit of a menace. I kind of understand why Ginger calls him the devil-bunny.

First thing this morning, Ginger and I get off the bus and run to the classroom. Mrs. Cavitch tells us that Cuddle Bunny had an adventure last night. He escaped his cage again – that rabbit's like Houdini or something – and he even escaped the classroom when Mrs. Cavitch got here this morning. Can you believe it?

Luckily, they caught him pretty fast and he's back home safe and sound, but he made a mess in the classroom last night.

The floor is covered in silver strips of shiny paper. "What's all the silver stuff?" Ginger asks.

Mrs. Cavitch shows us the chewed-up yogurt chip bag. It's mostly silver, but someone had chewed on it in the night. It's covered in bite marks and tiny holes.

"Did Cuddles do that?" I wonder.

"He must have," Mrs. Cavitch says. "This was almost full yesterday, but now it's completely empty."

"Wow," I say. "He must have been really hungry."

"That rabbit'll eat anything," Ginger says. "I don't think he has to be hungry at all. He just has to be alive."

I laugh out loud.

Ginger smiles a tiny smile.

"The bag wasn't even near the cage when I found it," Mrs. Cavitch says. "It was over there, by the bookshelf." She points toward the back of the classroom.

"Cuddles sure was busy last night," I say.

"Hey, where's our tiger?" Ginger suddenly asks, walking toward the back counter where our school mascot usually sits.

Before Mrs. Cavitch can answer, Ginger comes to a sudden stop and wails, "Oh no! Mrs. Cavitch, look." She reaches down and picks something up.

She turns to face us. She's holding our tiger, but he's a real mess. His nose is missing, some stuffing is falling from the side of his tummy and his mouth looks lopsided.

"That devil-bunny did this, didn't he?" Ginger demands.

Mrs. Cavitch sighs. She takes the tiger from Ginger and tells her that she'll work on sewing up Tiger later. She sets the tiger on her desk and starts to write on the front board.

Ginger's eyes widen. "If he did that to our tiger, what do you suppose he did to my hat?" She bolts for the closet.

I race after her.

The minute we reach the closet, my stomach drops.

There's a mess of scraps in the middle of the floor. For a terrible moment, I'm afraid it's Ginger's hat, but then I realize the scraps are mostly blue and Ginger's hat is purple.

"What is that?" Ginger asks.

"I don't know." I approach the mess slowly. I crouch down and study it. "It looks like a sweatshirt. Maybe."

"Oh, wow," Ginger says. "Didn't I tell you he's a devil-bunny? I mean look at that. I'm glad that's not my sweatshirt. Someone's gonna be awfully mad."

I nod. "Maybe we should move it."

"Maybe we should throw it away."

I'm doubtful. "I don't know. It's not ours."

"Here." Ginger drags over a box of magazines that we sometimes use for class projects. "Put it in here."

I scoop up the mess and drop it in the box.

Ginger wrinkles her nose. "I don't know why we're keeping it," she says. "No one's gonna want to wear that."

"Yeah, but at least they'll know what happened to it this way," I tell her, "instead of wondering where it went."

She nods.

I stand up. "At least it wasn't your hat."

"Yeah," Ginger says slowly, staring at something behind me.

I turn and see that her hat is sitting on the shelf in the closet, exactly where Ginger left it the day before.

"There, see?" I say. "Your hat's still there, all safe and sound."

She reaches up and slowly pulls down the hat. My eyes widen as I get a good look at it. I'm not sure, but it doesn't look exactly right.

Ginger stands there a minute, then says, "I knew it, I knew it, I knew it!" She storms out of the closet and heads for the bunny cage.

I race after her.

"Look what you did," she tells the rabbit, who's happily eating veggies and not even looking at her. "Look!" she shakes the hat at the cage, but the rabbit doesn't even move.

"What's wrong, Ginger?" Mrs. Cavitch asks.

"Look at my hat, Mrs. Cavitch," Ginger says. "It was on the shelf in the closet and that devil-bunny still got to it!"

"I don't think the bunny can jump that high, Ginger," I protest.

"Of course it can. How else is that bunny getting free? Because he's talented, that's how."

"Well," I begin, not certain what I'm going to say, when Mrs. Cavitch interrupts us.

"Let me see your hat, Ginger."

She hands it over.

"It's not that bad, sweetheart. The lace and flowers got dislodged a little, that's all. I'll work on wrapping them and re-attaching them this afternoon. It'll be just fine, good as new tomorrow. I promise."

"Are you sure?" Ginger asks. "I don't want that bunny touching my things anymore."

"I'm sure, sweetheart. Cuddles has already had a very eventful morning, so I think he'll just stay in his cage for recess today."

Thump! Thump! Thump!

We all jump and stare at the cage.

Cuddles is glaring at us as if he understood what Mrs. Cavitch said.

Mrs. Cavitch laughs. "I just love it when he does that. Isn't it the cutest thing ever?"

Thump! Cuddles slams his feet to the floor, making a sound that reverberates through the room.

Ginger giggles.

Thump!

Cuddles leaps for his house, disappears inside it, then –

Thump! Thump!

Maria

MRS. CAVITCH TELLS us the story of Cuddles' adventures last night. I decide to write about those for our writing assignment. That bunny sure is funny.

I ask Mrs. Cavitch if I can type my story into the computer and she agrees. When I turn on the computer and try to log in, the keyboard doesn't work. Nothing I type shows up on the screen.

I switch computers. I turn it on and try again. This time, the mouse doesn't work.

I raise my hand. Mrs. Cavitch comes over and I tell her the problem.

She checks the mouse cord to make sure it's plugged in, but when she pulls on the cord, it's broken in two! And it has teeth marks all over it.

She checks the other computers and it's the same thing.

"Did Cuddles do that?" I ask.

"I'm afraid so," she says. "It's a good thing he didn't chew one of the power cords. He could have been electrocuted."

I gasp. Poor Cuddles! That would be terrible. "I can stay inside with him, Mrs. Cavitch. I don't mind. I'll watch him to make sure he doesn't chew anything bad. I'll take real good care of him."

Mrs. Cavitch smiles. "Thank you, Maria, but I don't think that will be necessary. Cuddles has had enough adventures for one day. I think he'll be staying in his cage for recess."

Poor Cuddles. It must be terrible to be locked up all day long.

Mrs. Cavitch manages to find a keyboard and a mouse that haven't been chewed and she gets me set up on a working computer.

I type my story into the computer and I add the part about Cuddles risking his life to chew our computer cords. He's such a darling little bunny.

*

After lunch, Mrs. Cavitch tells us she took pictures of Cuddles during our recess yesterday and asks if we want to see them.

"Yes, please, Mrs. Cavitch," the class choruses.

Mrs. Cavitch turns on the projector and opens her laptop. Soon she has pictures of Cuddle Bunny up on the screen. The pictures are so cool. I remember when Cuddle Bunny escaped and raced around the room and how he scared Ginger. He sure did jump high then, but this time – wow! He's way high in the air in some of the pictures. He seems so happy.

I don't know why he likes Ginger so much when she doesn't like him. It makes me so mad. He sleeps in her backpack, but ignores mine. He stares at her hat all day, but when her hat is next to my backpack, he doesn't visit either one.

Now Mrs. Cavitch is showing a video of him

running and playing, and guess whose desk he doesn't go near at all? Mine. And guess whose desk he runs around three times in a row, making everyone laugh? Ginger's.

It's not fair. Why does he like her so much?

Wow. He's moving so fast, I can't believe it. I'd fall on my face, if I tried to turn and go in the opposite direction like that.

"Cuddles is like the Olympics Rabbit or something," I announce to the class.

Everyone agrees. Except for Ginger. She just stares at the screen with a weird look on her face.

She probably wishes Cuddle Bunny would leave her desk alone. She's such a meanie!

Tyrabbisaurus Rex

IS THAT REALLY what I look like? I turn and stare at the picture of me on the wall, my giant Tyrabbisaurus Rex picture, then compare that to the pictures on the screen. I don't really look the same at all. In the picture on the wall, I'm brown and fierce looking, but in the pictures Mrs. Cabbage is showing, I'm white. And fluffy. And kind of *cuddly*. That is so not cool.

I don't believe her. It's a trick. I'm not cuddly and I'm not fluffy.

I am a Tyrabbisaurus Rex, people – a T-Rex and I

roaaarrrr at you with the power of my mind.

I turn and storm into my house where I stomp my feet a couple times, then hunker down to sulk.

"I'm not sure Cuddles is the right name for our rabbit, Mrs. Cabbage," someone says.

My nose twitches and I lift my head a little. Finally – someone's listening.

"Why do you say that, Jonathan?" Mrs. Cabbage asks.

"Because he's standing like a dinosaur in that picture."

I poke my head out of the house, hoping to see a picture of me looking big and brown and fierce, but instead it's just cuddly, little me standing on my hind legs. I still have those long floppy ears and I don't look scary at all.

"A dinosaur?" Mrs. Cabbage says.

I have no idea what a dinosaur is, but it sounds lame. I'm not a dinosaur, I shout at them with the power of my mind. I'm a Tyrabbisaurus –

"Yeah, like a T-Rex." Jonathan points to my poster.

"He's right," Derek exclaims. "Cuddle Bunny's standing just like a T-Rex!"

Of course I'm standing like a T-Rex. I am one. Maybe they're finally getting it.

"Plus he's always stamping his feet," Zing says, "like he's mad at us or something."

I stamp my feet again, just because I can.

"And he's kind of mean," Ginger mutters. "He's always ruining my things."

What kind of gratitude is that? It's a supreme, Tyrabbisaurus Rex-sized compliment to nibble on someone's clothing or hats. It's like she doesn't even realize how much I admire her.

"Oh my gosh," Maria squeals. "He's a T-Rab! Mrs. Cabbage, he's a T-Rab!"

Huh. That's kind of cool.

"Yeah," the other kids start shouting their agreement. "He is."

I come out of my house and stand at the cage door. The kids are all talking excitedly about my name and how Cuddle Bunny doesn't fit.

"He's totally a T-Rab," Jonathan says. "Can we call him that, Mrs. Cabbage? Please?"

Wow. These kids really get me. I'm not a Cuddles at all and they know it.

"Well, I don't know. What if Cuddles likes his name?"

Seriously? This woman is too much. I've been telling her for weeks that I'm not a Cuddle Bunny, but she still doesn't understand.

"Let's ask him," Javon says.

"Yeah, we can ask him," Derek says and the rest of the class agrees.

"Well, all right," Mrs. Cabbage says. "We can try." She walks over to my cage. "Hello, my cuddly bunny-kins," she croons.

Ugh. I stamp my feet at her.

"Don't you want to keep your name, Cuddles? Don't you want to be our little Cuddle Bunny?"

I storm into my house and stamp my feet again. What is wrong with this human?

"What about T-Rab?" Mrs. Cabbage asks.

I stick my head out of the house and stare at her.

"Do you want to be called T-Rab?"

I scream yes at her with the power of my mind, but as usual she can't hear anything. I come out of the house and stare at her.

"That's a yes, isn't it, Mrs. Cabbage?" Derek asks.

"I think so, Derek."

"Yeah!" The kids cheer.

So do I, but as usual, they can't hear me.

It doesn't matter though because I have a new, super-awesome, fearsome name. I am Tyrabbisaurus Rex, but you can call me T-Rab.

Veggie-awesome.

T-Rab

THE HUMANS ARE all gone. First the students leave, then a little while later, the teacher-warden croons a bunch of nonsense my way. "Bye-bye, cuddly bunnykins." She flops her hand around like a crazy person, snaps off the lights, closes the door and click-clacks away. I don't understand humans. They're just weird.

But now it's quiet. No one's in the room but me. Just me. Tyrabbisaurus Rextraordinaire. About to embark upon my most dangerous mission yet. That's right.

You guessed it. Prison break time! And this time, I won't forget to actually escape.

I poke my head out of my house and glance around. No one's staring at me. All is quiet. The mission is a go!

I barrel out of my house and down the first ramp, where I hunker low and glower around the corner of the ramp. Nothing to impede my way. I'm off!

I race around and down the second ramp. As I hit the bottom floor, I screech to a halt, my highly intelligent brain cells blaring a warning. Someone is coming!

I hunker as low as I can and stare at the door across the room. Is the teacher-warden returning? Has she already discovered my attempt to escape? I haven't even left the cage yet. How could she know?

The knob on the classroom door begins to turn. Slowly, slowly and then with a quiet squeeeeak, the door is opened and a human enters. It's not the teacher-warden.

It's a man with whiskers like mine. That's weird. I didn't know humans could have whiskers. Maybe he's just another Tyrabbisaurus Rex in disguise.

I stare closely, but no. I don't think he's a T-Rex. I'm still the only prisoner in this place and it's my duty to all T-Rexes everywhere to launch my escape as soon as – what's that sound? It's horrible, awful, my ears, my ears!

I race up and up, and into my house I barrel.

Wroooo-wroooo-wrooo-wroooo.

The sound goes on and on and on. These humans are horrible creatures. They cannot convince me to enjoy this captivity and so they torture me with the sound of a thousand demons. Have they come to eat my tail? Have they come to feast upon my ears? Are they going to steal my fierce claws?

It's not right, I tell you. That horrific, demonic machine is not going to steal my tail. No it won't! I am a fierce Tyrabbisaurus Rex and I will make it stop.

I glower at the machine as it whirls around the room, *wroo-wroo-wroo-wroo-wrooing* everywhere. I scream at it with the power of my mind, *Stop, you evil contraption. Stop!*

I cannot believe it.

I've been communicating with humans for months now and not a single human can understand even one of my words, but the machine of death does. When I yell stop, it actually stops.

Do you know what this means?

It means machines are smarter than humans. I had no idea humans were so dumb. Sure, I knew they weren't very smart, but I didn't realize it was this bad. I mean, they've got to be the stupidest beings on the planet, if even machines are smarter than them.

The whiskered human grumbles and shakes the machine, but it doesn't start up again.

Thank goodness that monstrous sound is over. I glower at the machine, telling it with my thought rays that its evil days are over. I don't think the machine believes me though. It's wagging its long tail at me.

No, wait.

The machine isn't wagging its tail. Didn't I tell you humans are weird? This just proves it.

The *human* is wagging and pulling the machine's tail. I hope he doesn't plan to pull my tail like that. I'll have to bite his fingers if he does.

The machine's tail is awfully long, but that doesn't stop the whiskered human. He just keeps pulling it and pulling it, and then you will never believe what he does next. He sticks the end of the tail into the wall! And then… *wroo-wroo-wroo-wroo-wroo-wroo*! Why me?

I stare at the machine as the human drags it all over the floor.

Wait. What is he doing?

He's coming toward my cage! Why is he bringing that monster over here?

The human stops in front of my cage and leaning down, puts his big, whiskered face right in front of my cage door. I stamp my foot to tell the human to go away, but he ignores me. Why don't these humans understand that I am a fierce Tyrabbisaurus Rex who will bite their noses off if they keep sticking them in my cage?

The human opens my cage door, pulls a giant tube from the machine and sticks it into my cage.

Wrooo-wrooo-wrooo-wrooo-wroooo!

I bolt out of my house and go flying down the ramp. As I race down, I can feel the air from that monster-machine ruffling my fur.

I reach the middle floor and see that monster tube thing heading for the second cage door. I bolt past the door on the second floor and race down the ramp to the bottom floor. I stand there at the bottom of the ramp and stare back up it. As I watch, the long tube thing scrabbles around at the top of the ramp. I don't know what that thing is doing, but it is just wrong. It's so loud!

Wrooo-wrooo-wrooo-wrooo-wrooo!

The tube disappears, but I don't look away. I can still hear it *wrooing* and I know it hasn't gone away. It's going to come back. Any minute now. Any minute.

Argh! Something flashes by me. I whirl around. The tube is in the cage on the bottom floor now, right in front of me.

Before my very eyes, it sucks up some of my hay. My yummy hay that I was saving for later. That evil machine stole my hay.

I am so mad that I stamp my feet.

Wroooo-wroooo-wroooooo!

That machine is so rude. *Stop that!* I mind-roar at the machine, but this time, it ignores me.

I'm about to roar at it again, or maybe bite its sucky face off when all of a sudden, I notice something.

The bottom cage door is open.

The tube thing is just sitting there, not moving anymore, and the human is turned away, talking to a silver box.

Don't ask me why. Humans are weird.

While his back is turned, I leap for freedom. Yes! I'm free. I race into the closet, headed for the beautiful, puppy-nest I made last night. Imagine my surprise when I discover my nest is gone. Why do these things keep happening to me? Now I have to make a new one.

Looking around the closet, I notice something purple on the floor. It looks like a flower. I nibble on it a bit. Delicious!

The flower has a tail, only it's sticking straight up. I look up and notice it's really long. I nibble on the tail and then I tug on it a bit. Something high above me moves. I stare, then scratch at the tail, pulling at it just a little.

Whoosh!

A rush of purple comes flying toward me.

I dart away.

The purple explodes onto the floor. It's awesome!

Purple tails and flowers everywhere. I move forward to check it out.

It's the giant hat the little girl with the yummy pink dress was wearing. She has the best things ever.

I scrabble at the long scarf-tail and nibble my way around the entire thing. The scarf thing tastes pretty good, but the flowers are awesome and the best part? Right in the center of this mass of purple is a giant hollowed-out burrow just waiting for me to make a nest of purple tails and flowers inside. It's true!

The burrow's where the little girl kept her head (I told you humans are weird), but I'm going to use it for its intended purpose – nest-building!

I get started right away.

I scrabble at the purple scarf-things and drag them into the burrow. I scratch them into place, then drag some flowers into my burrow too. I eat a few of the petals because I just can't resist. Yummy!

I nibble, pull and tug until everything's in the perfect spot. I spin around three times, testing everything out, before finally settling down.

Aw, sweet comfort.

My beautiful, purple nest is awesome. The best. Nest. Ever.

*

Crash!

I leap to my feet, abandoning my nest to dart behind a box that's sitting in the closet.

Someone's in the outer room.

"Mrs. Cabbage, did you fix my hat?" It's the little girl

with the awesome things, the one called Ginger – isn't that a kind of food? I think it is. Maybe even it's a vegetable. She doesn't look like a vegetable.

"I sure did," Mrs. Cabbage says. "I put it back on the shelf in the closet."

I peek out the closet door.

Ginger and Derek are standing by Mrs. Cabbage's desk.

"Thanks, Mrs. Cabbage," Ginger says. She and Derek head for the closet.

Is she coming for my nest? It used to be her hat, but now it's my nest and I spent a lot of time making it perfect. She's not going to take it, is she?

I dart over to the nest and grab it with my teeth. I try to pull it behind the box, but it's too heavy.

"I'm starving." I hear Derek's voice.

"I'm just going to check on my hat and then we can go to breakfast, okay?"

"Fine."

They're right outside the closet door.

I stare at the door, then at my nest. I have no choice. I abandon my nest and dart behind the box again.

"Oh, no!" Ginger's really loud.

"What's wrong?" Derek asks.

"My hat!" Ginger collapses next to my nest and picks it up.

Derek settles at her side. "Wow," he says.

"It's the last hat my mom gave me, Derek, and now it's ruined." She bursts into tears.

I didn't mean to make Ginger cry.

It's just her hat was so pretty. It made a perfect nest.

I hop out from behind the box.

Derek puts an arm around her and hugs her. "It's okay, Ginger. I'm sure your mom will understand."

Ginger shakes her head, crying quietly. "But it's the last gift she gave me, right before she died. She won't ever give me another hat and Cuddles ruined it."

Derek's silent for a minute then he says, "My dad died too. I was a baby, so I don't really remember him. The only thing I have from him is a teddy bear he bought for me the day I was born."

I don't remember my parents either. I hop a little closer.

"You don't remember your dad?" Ginger says.

Derek shakes his head.

"That's so sad," Ginger says. "At least I remember all

the good times with my mom, that she loved me and played with me."

"Yeah. My mom tells me about him, how happy he was to be a dad, but it's not the same as remembering him myself."

Ginger nods. She picks up a purple flower – it's one that I nibbled on the night before, so it looks a little lopsided. She bows her head and a couple more tears streak down her face.

I hop the last distance to her and set my front paws on her leg.

She doesn't notice me so I nudge her with my nose.

She pulls away and gasps.

I hop into her lap and circle around a couple times before I settle down.

"Wow," Derek says.

I lean forward and nudge her hand with my nose.

"What does that mean?" Ginger asks.

I nudge her again.

"Maybe you should pet him," Derek suggests.

Ginger hesitantly strokes my head. It feels pretty good. I close my eyes and relax.

"Look at that. He must like you an awful lot," Derek says.

That's probably going a bit far. A nudge could mean so many things. It could mean hey, you, feed me. Or you're kind of stupid, but I forgive you. Or even I love you more than carrot tops. Probably not though. Nothing was better than carrot tops.

In this case, nudging Ginger was just my way of saying I'm sorry, but as usual, the humans don't understand me. Instead they think it means I like

Ginger, which must be why she decides to pet me. I won't complain though because she's really good at this petting thing.

I relax and listen to the two of them whisper together. Derek shares what his mom has told him about his father and Ginger shares her memories of her mother and the two of them make me feel happy, almost like I'm at home with my T-Rab family.

Maybe I'll adopt them. Ginger can be my adopted Tyrabbisaurus mom and Derek can be my adopted Tyrabbisaurus dad. That sounds like a perfect plan.

I lay there imagining the two of them in Tyrabbisaurus bodies when suddenly someone comes along and scoops me up.

"All right, Mister T-Rab, I don't know how you keep getting out, but enough is enough." And Mrs. Cabbage shoves me back in my cage.

This time I don't mind that much, though, because I'm tired and hungry. And veggies are waiting for me in my bowl.

I pounce on the first veggie I see – it's a carrot top of veggie-awesomeness – and I drag it into my house to devour its yummy goodness.

*

I never should have let Mrs. Cabbage catch me. I've been bored ever since she scooped me up ten thousand hours ago.

First I take a nap because that's what T-Rabs do after having amazing adventures and building awesome nests. And speaking of nests, can you believe they didn't put my nest in the cage with me?

Instead, Ginger gives my nest to Mrs. Cabbage, who says she'll try to fix it again.

Fix it? I roar at her. *Are you crazy? It's perfect!*

"All we need is some new ribbon and maybe a few new flowers," she tells Ginger. Now that doesn't sound too bad. More ribbon and more flowers – yummy. "I'll get what we need and work on it this weekend. With a bit of glue, it'll be good as new."

Glue? Why would they want to put glue on my nest? I glower at them suspiciously. Is she talking about ruining all my hard work when she says it'll be good as new? It's perfectly new now. I made it that way on purpose!

Ginger's finally stopped crying, though, and she

doesn't look as sad as she did before.

I didn't mean to make her feel bad. I guess it's okay if they ruin my nest.

I look around the room. I'll just have to build another one. I spend about seventy-two hours plotting where I can build my nest and what I can use to build it.

There's a box full of paper that looks like it might be fun to pull out and shred. I never noticed that box before. That's the great thing about my bunny palace – yes, I've decided not to call this place they've locked me in a cage anymore. It's my palace. My T-Rab palace and it has three levels and when I'm on the top level, it's like I'm king of the world and I can see everything.

I can see the box that's almost full where kids are always putting their paper. I can hop into it easy, knock it over and scrabble all around.

I plot how I'll pull the papers out and shred them into tiny bits and how I'll eat some of them because paper – yum! Then I plot how I'll pull them onto that bookshelf there and build me a little nest. I'll use that paperback book – the pages look yummy plus they'll make good material for my nest.

I'll also use the pillow in the reading nook. It looks really comfortable. I haven't slept on it yet. I need to try it out next time I'm free.

And that tiger's eyes. So he can't stare at me anymore. I'll nibble away the black threads of his eyes and then whatever's left after I'm done nibbling, I'll put in my nest to snack on later.

What else can I use?

The teacher's desk looks mighty interesting. It's covered in papers and pencils and –

Ooooh, hay. Yummy.

Chomp, chomp, chomp.

I wonder what that book'll taste like. The one on the teacher's desk. It's much, much bigger than any book I've ever seen. It's like the king of all books. It has wire, spirally things on the end that look fun. I'll chew those and I'll nibble some of the pages and maybe I'll even sleep on top of it. It's so huge, I bet five T-Rabs could curl up on it and still have room left over. Well, maybe not five. Maybe, three. Okay, maybe just me. But definitely me. Stretched out on top of that book, chewing on the spiral, snoozing away, enjoying the lovely freedom.

That sounds so great, I take a nap, right on top of the hay I've been eating.

When I wake up the kids are gone. Now where did they go? They left me all alone again.

I stamp my feet.

"What's the matter, bunny-boo?" Mrs. Cabbage asks.

Well, that's all right then. I'm not completely alone.

"Everyone's out at recess."

Recess, yes! I stand in front of the door to my cage and stare at her expectantly. It's freedom time!

Mrs. Cabbage laughs. "Not today, Mr. Bunny-kins."

What? What does she mean not today?

"You already had your recess running down the hallway."

No, I did not. That wasn't recess, that was an escape. Doesn't she know the difference? How can she be so mean to me?

I stamp my feet at her, but she just giggles.

Argh. I storm into my house and stamp my feet again.

The kids come back, but it's a long, boring afternoon because no one lets me out to play. I take another nap because I'm just that bored.

The kids leave for the day and Mrs. Cabbage gives me a treat and some pellet food (which isn't as good as the veggies or the yogurt treats), but it's okay. Then she leaves me too, but you know what she does before she leaves?

She checks all three latches on my bunny palace!

First she checks the top one. She pulls on it and says, "That's good. All nice and tight." Then she pulls the latch on the second and third floors too. "Well, Mr. T-Rab, looks like you're all bundled up safe and sound for the night, so I'll see you tomorrow. I love you, my bunny-boo."

She turns out the lights, waves and then she disappears through the doors.

I check all three latches right off. She's right, they're locked tight.

I chew on them, but nothing happens.

I stamp my feet. My bunny palace has a few flaws in it.

Oooh – parsley. How'd that get down here? Yummy-licious. Must have dropped it down the ramp. I love it when that happens.

I finish my unexpected treat and look around. I hop

to the door of the cage and stare out into the darkened classroom.

That tiger's still out there. He's stalking me, pacing around my bunny palace, trying to figure out a way in.

Well, ha! I tell him. *The drawbridge is up and my bunny palace is secure. No tigers allowed here.*

The tiger doesn't answer me. He never does. But I know he's mad.

He's trying to get in, but I won't let him. He has spies everywhere. All those desks, staring at me with their beady little eyes, trying to figure out a way in. *Ha! Not gonna happen,* I tell them.

I spend about ten trillion hours pacing up and down the ramps, guarding the three levels of my bunny palace.

I also eat a lot of hay and I chew on my litter box. It doesn't really do anything to it, but I like the teeth marks I leave behind.

I also chew on my house. It's made of wood and it kind of tastes yummy. Maybe if I work at it hard enough, I can add a window to my house.

On the bottom ramp, I discover someone left behind something that looks suspiciously like a wooden rattle.

Seriously. It looks like a rattle. For babies.

I sneer at the rattle, then turn and shout at the tiger, *Very funny! Like I'm going to play with a rattle. You're just jealous because I'm inside this bunny palace and you're locked out there. So ha!*

I turn and storm up the ramp.

After about ten thousand hours of nothing to do, I go back to the rattle and stare at it. It's a wooden rod and it has a ring on it. It looks like good chewing material. I'm not going to play with it, of course, because I'm not a baby, but I might decide to eat it. Because it doesn't belong here.

I pounce on it.

It skitters across the floor.

Come back, you! I pounce on it again.

The little ring thing slides to the bottom of the rattle and just sits there. I toss my head and the rattle goes flying.

It lands at the bottom of the ramp.

I jump after it, grab it with my teeth and drag it up the ramp. I toss it into a corner on the second floor and stand there, staring at it.

Where to chew first?

The ring has possibilities.

I get my teeth around one end of it and I shake it hard.

I settle down beside the rattle and chew on the ring. I keep flipping the rattle up so that it turns and I can get at the other side of the ring.

Even though I chew on that rattle for something like ninety-seven thousand hours, it doesn't ever get any smaller.

I think it's a magical rattle. It's impervious to my

fierce Tyrabbisaurus Rex teeth. Well, we'll see about that!

I chew on it and I nap, then I have some hay, then I chew on my rattle again.

I drag it up the ramp and down the ramp and all over my bunny palace. I'm determined to break the spell that protects this rattle from my teeth of doom.

Finally, after a long night of battling the magical properties protecting that rattle, I place the rattle on the second floor of my palace, then plop down on top of it.

It's my rattle, I yell at the tiger, *and you can't have it. I will figure out what enchantment you placed on this rattle and I will chew it into oblivion. You'll never get it back. Ha!* And then I give an evil laugh with the power of my mind, but the tiger doesn't reply.

He's stubborn, that tiger is.

Ginger

I CAN'T STOP thinking about Cuddles.

T-Rab. I have to remember that name. It's way better than Cuddles.

I wonder what T-Rab's up to today. Whatever it is, it probably isn't good because nothing he ever does is. First he poops on my dress, then he chews on my

Trixie Belden book, and then he ruins my hat. That rabbit sure does like my stuff.

The bus pulls up in front of me and I get on board. All the kids stare at me. It's probably because it's another jeans and t-shirt day. The third day in a row when I don't wear a dress. The second day in a row when I don't even have a hat.

I am wearing my mom's scarf though, the special one she gave me at our last tea party, the party we had to hold in her bed because she was too sick to get up. I almost didn't wear the scarf because that rabbit's determined to make me mad and my scarf might look tempting to him. But no rabbit's gonna keep me from wearing my mama's scarf.

I'll give up my tea-party dresses and maybe even the hats, but not my scarves.

I sit down on one of the empty seats and ignore all the kids staring at me.

"How come you're not wearing a hat today, Ginger?" Maria turns and sits up on her knees so she's staring at me over the seat in front of me.

I shrug.

"I liked the hat you wore the other day."

"I liked it too," I mutter. "But that dumb bunny ruined it."

"He did?" Maria asks.

"Uh-huh."

Derek leans across the aisle. "That's because he loves your stuff, Ginger."

I shrug.

"He does. He keeps going to your things because they probably smell like you, which means he must like you too."

Is Derek right? The rabbit does keep going to my things. My dress, my backpack, my desk, my hat. I remember the way the bunny looked when he poked his head out of my backpack. He twitched his nose at me. It made me jump, but really when I think about it now, it was kind of cute.

"And yesterday, he came right up to you," Derek says. "He put his paws on your leg and nudged you with his nose. I read that's how bunnies give kisses."

"Cuddle Bunny kissed you?" Maria wails. "When did that happen?"

"Yesterday morning," I tell her. "When we discovered my hat. He completely ruined it."

"Yeah, but he felt bad," Derek reminds me. "And his name's T-Rab," he tells Maria.

"I know, but I still like Cuddle Bunny too. Because he's so cuddly. Besides, how do you know he felt bad?" Maria asks.

"Because he came up to her when she was crying, nudged her and climbed onto her lap. It was so cute."

"He climbed onto your lap?" Maria gasps.

I nod.

Maria turns around and flops down on her seat. She doesn't say anything more for the entire bus ride, which is fine with me.

I have a lot to think about. I have to figure out if Derek's right. Is it possible the bunny's doing all these things because he likes me, not because he's being mean?

I stare out the window and think about T-Rab, the not-so-cuddly bunny.

Maria

IT'S NOT FAIR!

I flop down in my seat. That bunny is so cute and he's always going to Ginger instead of me. He even likes her hat more than my backpack.

Ginger doesn't even like rabbits. I do. I love Cuddle Bunny and he won't come near me!

I glare out the window as we roll up to the school. That darn bunny. No more Señorita Nice. I'm going to make him be my friend and that's that.

Ginger

"GOOD MORNING, GINGER," Mrs. Cavitch says as I enter the classroom. "Why aren't you at breakfast, dear?"

"I wanted to ask – I mean. Would it be okay if I pet T-Rab?" I say my words all in a rush so that I can't chicken out.

Mrs. Cavitch has a surprised look on her face. "Why, Ginger, I didn't think you liked the rabbit."

I shrug, not sure what to say.

"Of course, you can pet him." Mrs. Cavitch puts her arm around my shoulders and hugs me tight. She then takes my hand in hers. "Come along, dear." She walks me to the cage.

She does that a lot. Treats me different. All the teachers do. Ever since my mom died. I could probably ask Mrs. Cavitch for something really important, like not take a big test, and she'd say okay just because she feels sorry for me.

"Now T-Rab's a little out of sorts this morning," Mrs. Cavitch said. "I think he's mad at us because we didn't let him out once yesterday, plus I made sure the cage doors were all securely latched before leaving last night."

T-Rab pops his head out of his house.

Does he understand?

After a minute, he hops out of the house and stands right in front of the cage door, staring at us.

Mrs. Cavitch opens the door, reaches into the cage and scoops T-Rab out in one quick move. One minute he's in the cage and the next he's in her arms. She's amazing.

She faces me and smiles. "Go ahead, sweetie. Pet him."

I reach out and touch his back. He's so soft. I pet him gently and when he doesn't move, I inch my hand upward. I want to touch his ears. They're so floppy. I lift one ear up and it's even softer than his fur. I stroke it gently and giggle because it feels funny.

T-Rab turns his head and twitches his nose at me. I giggle again because he looks so silly. Then I gently stroke his tiny nose. His whiskers quiver.

"He's so soft," I say to Mrs. Cavitch.

"He sure is. Would you like to hold him?"

I hesitate. Would I?

T-Rab nudges my hand with his nose.

I giggle and nod my head quick before I change my mind.

"Okay, sweetie. Let's go sit on the floor over here." Mrs. Cavitch leads me to the reading area and has me sit criss-cross applesauce on the floor. She settles T-Rab in my lap.

I think T-Rab will probably hop away immediately,

but instead he paws at my jeans a little then curls up with his head on my left knee.

I stare down at him. He's just lying there, draped across my left leg. I think – I think he fell asleep. I lean over and stare at his face.

His eyes are closed. His nose twitches and his whiskers quiver, but he doesn't move. He's asleep. He fell asleep on my lap! I can't believe it.

I straighten up and look around the classroom.

Mrs. Cavitch is busy writing on the front board. The clock says 7:35. The other kids will be here soon.

I look back at T-Rab. He's still sleeping.

I hesitate then carefully settle one hand on his back. His back moves up and down as he breathes. I pet him slowly.

He doesn't wake up. He just keeps sleeping and I keep petting him and I think that maybe, just maybe T-Rab does like me. Not just a little, but maybe a whole lot, just like Derek said.

Maria

GINGER ISN'T AT breakfast. I don't know where that girl went. She just disappeared after we got to school. Maybe she got kidnapped.

A couple days ago, I heard the office ladies talking about a rat in the hallway. Maybe the rat ate her.

I look around the cafeteria. She's definitely not here.

I get up and head for the trash can. It's right by the cafeteria door.

I dump my trash and look around. No one's

watching.

I'm a rabbit. I'm a rabbit. No one sees me because I'm a rabbit.

I walk to the cafeteria door, push it open and slip through the opening.

The door closes behind me.

I stand in the hallway and listen. No one comes after me.

It worked!

I pretended to be a rabbit and no one even noticed when I left the cafeteria.

Maybe Mrs. Cavitch will let me hold Cuddles if I visit before school begins.

I skip down the hallway.

Mrs. Cavitch

"MRS. CAVITCH?"

I turn and look at the door. Little Maria's standing just inside the classroom looking at me.

"Well, good morning, Maria. How are you today?"

"Okay. Mrs. Cavitch, can I maybe hold Cuddle Bunny for a little bit?" Maria asks her question in one huge rush, the words tumbling over the top of one another.

I really shouldn't encourage the students to come early. Once the girls tell the other students, none of them will want to eat breakfast. They'll all be visiting me before school begins, hoping to hold Cuddle Bunny.

I glance toward the reading nook where Ginger is sitting quietly with Cuddle Bunny in her lap. They look so cute. I need to take a picture of them together.

"Mrs. Cavitch?"

I look back at Maria. "Of course you may, Maria. You have to be quiet though. Cuddle Bunny is sound asleep in Ginger's lap."

Maria's eyes widen, then she frowns. "Ginger's here too?" She looks toward the reading nook, apparently noticing Ginger for the first time.

"She sure is. You girls must have had the same idea. Come on then." I lead Maria over to where Ginger is sitting.

Maria plops down in front of Ginger.

"Hi, Maria," Ginger whispers, still staring down at Cuddles. "You should pet him. He's so soft. Here."

She lifts her hand from Cuddle Bunny's back, reaches for Maria's hand and places it on Cuddles. "Pet him."

Maria smiles and gently strokes Cuddles.

I take a couple pictures of the girls as they stare down at Cuddles, whispering to each other about how soft he is. The three of them together, the two girls' heads touching as they lean over the rabbit is one of the most beautiful pictures I've ever taken.

I think I'll call it Friendship.

T-Rab

THIS IS THE best feeling ever.

Warm.

Safe.

Sleepy.

My humans aren't so bad, really. They know just how to hold a T-Rab and how to pet me so my fur is all silky-smooth. They even like to play with my ears, petting them and making me feel super-awesome.

It almost makes me forget how loud they can be.

Jonathan

"LET'S GO," DEREK hisses. "The coast is clear." He drags me out of the bathroom and pulls me down the hallway.

"Where are we going, Derek? I'm hungry you know. The cafeteria's back that way."

"I want to visit T-Rab."

"But what about breakfast?"

"Mrs. Cavitch'll give us a snack if we ask her. I want to see the rabbit."

"Fine," I sigh as Derek leads me to the classroom door.

We get there and Derek stops. He shoves me forward. "You ask her."

"What? This was your idea!" I say.

"Yeah, but I already got to pet the rabbit yesterday morning. You didn't, so she'll probably say yes if you ask."

"Fine." I open the door and we walk in. "Mrs. Cavitch?"

"Good morning, boys."

"We were wondering if we could pet T-Rab," I say.

"I suppose that would be fine. Go hang up your things, then you can join Ginger and Maria in the reading area."

I look over and realize the girls beat us here. They're sitting against some pillows and T-Rab is in Ginger's lap! "I thought Ginger hated the rabbit," I whisper to Derek.

"Who cares?" he says. "Come on!" He grabs my arm

and drags me into the closet.

We hang up our backpacks and I notice our box of magazines has a mess inside it. "Whoa, what's this?" I ask.

"Oh, T-Rab did that the other night."

"What is it?" I ask, tilting my head.

"I don't know. Maybe a shirt or something. Come on."

"Wait. I want to check this out." I lean over the box and start moving some of the strips of cloth. "It looks like there's an animal on it."

"What do you mean?" Derek leans over to see better.

"There. It's a tail." I move more of the strips. "And a body. It looks kind of like–"

"A puppy!" Derek says excitedly. "Who wore a puppy sweatshirt this week?"

My eyes widen. I grin and scoop up the sweatshirt.

Long strips of cloth fall off it into the box. The puppy's face is pretty much destroyed.

"Come on," I tell Derek.

"Hey, Maria." I walk out of the closet. "Isn't this your sweatshirt?" I hold it up.

Maria looks up from where she's leaning over T-Rab. She stares at me a minute, eyes round, then looks down at the bunny, then back at the sweatshirt.

"Oh, Maria," Ginger whispers. "Oh, no. T-Rab destroyed your puppy shirt."

Maria gets this really weird look on her face, then she jumps up and lets out a squeal. Everyone jumps in surprise, including T-Rab, who jerks to a standing position then twitches his nose at Maria.

"Oh my gosh, oh my gosh," Maria squeals. She races to me, grabs the sweatshirt, holds it up against her and spins in a circle.

"Look at my sweatshirt, look at it! T-Rab liked my sweatshirt. He liked it, he liked it!"

"Yeah, too much, if you ask me," I tell her. "Look at it, it's ruined."

"I know." Maria grins. "Isn't it beautiful?"

I look at Derek. We have no idea what to say. Because really, there's something wrong with that girl if she thinks her headless puppy sweatshirt is beautiful.

Ginger

I STARE AT Maria in shocked amazement. I just don't understand her at all. T-Rab completely destroyed her sweatshirt and she's ridiculously happy.

Derek sits beside me and bumps me with his shoulder.

"Hi," I whisper.

"Hey," he whispers back. He reaches out to scratch T-Rab's head.

"Look at Maria," I say. She's twirling around the room, dancing with her ruined sweatshirt. "I think she's kind of crazy, don't you?"

Derek laughs. "She just likes the bunny."

"Yeah," Jonathan says as he crouches down beside us. "An awful, awful lot."

T-Rab twitches an ear and Jonathan reaches out to pet him.

"Can I put my sweatshirt in T-Rab's cage, Mrs. Cavitch?" Maria asks.

T-Rab's ear lifts a bit and he stares at Mrs. Cavitch, as if he's waiting for her to answer too.

"Wow. Maria's really okay with you ruining her sweatshirt, T-Rab," I tell him.

"That's very generous of you, Maria," Mrs. Cavitch says, "but I don't think clothing is good for bunnies. The dyes might make him sick."

T-Rab's ear falls and his whiskers quiver.

He looks so disappointed.

I glance over at my hat. It's sitting on Mrs. Cavitch's desk. She promised to try to fix it over the weekend.

I look back down at T-Rab. He's so sad.

"What about my hat, Mrs. Cavitch?" I ask her.

Derek jerks a bit and stares at me. "Ginger?" he says.

I shrug. "He needs a nest."

"Well, I don't know." Mrs. Cavitch picks up my hat and looks at it. "The hat itself is made of straw so that should be okay. We'd have to remove the bits of scarf and flowers that are still attached and we'd have to make sure there aren't any threads that might make him sick."

"We can do that," I say.

"Are you sure, Ginger?" Derek asks. "It's the last hat your mom gave you."

"T-Rab needs it more. Besides I have other hats she gave me."

"I bet I can save some of the ribbon and flowers, Ginger," Mrs. Cavitch says. "We can make you a new hat or maybe a scarf with what I manage to save. What do you think?"

"That'd be great!"

"All right, then. We don't have time to take apart the hat this morning, but maybe during recess?"

I nod excitedly.

"I'll stay and help too," Maria says. She's wearing the puppy sweatshirt now. She looks silly because the puppy has no face and the sweatshirt is covered in slash marks, but she's happier than I've ever seen her and that's saying a lot because Maria's always happy.

"Us too," Jonathan says and Derek nods.

"Cool," I say. "Did you hear that, T-Rab? You get to keep my hat after all."

T-Rab

I THOUGHT RECESS would never come.

It's finally here, but does Mrs. Cabbage let me out of my palace to play? No, she does not.

She says it's because there's fabric and flowers on the floor.

Well, yeah, that's why I want out, people. The purple scarf and flowers are calling my name.

They look delicious.

And can I just say – I might like these kids, but they're definitely a little slow in the head, if you know what I mean. I just don't understand why they would ruin a perfectly good nest that way.

When Ginger told me I could keep her hat, I was so excited. I love her hat. Did I mention that it's purple? I love purple!

Only they're taking all the purple stuff off. The bits of lace, the vines and yummy-licious flowers – all gone. Even the giant scarf that I spent so much time taking off and then putting inside my nest. They shoved it and all the flower-treats I was saving for later into a giant bag. Why would they do that?

I need that stuff to make my nest perfect and for yummy snacks later! I yell at them.

Nobody even looks at me.

I stamp my feet at them, but they just giggle and keep pulling off vines and flowers.

So I stamp my feet again.

"Oh, what's the matter, T-Rab?" Ginger asks. "You're going to love this hat when we're finished with it."

Highly unlikely. Especially since they're ruining it.

"You don't want these flowers," Maria says.

Oh, yes, I do, I tell her, but she doesn't even look up.

She's busy working on two flowers that have been twined together and woven into the hat's brim. She's unwinding them and taking them off the hat. Why would she do that?

"They're not real flowers, T-Rab. You wouldn't like them at all."

Not real flowers? Who does she think she's kidding? I stamp my feet at her. *Those are too flowers. You can't fool me,* I tell her.

"Look, T-Rab," Ginger holds up a flower. "It's plastic."

I don't know what plastic is, but I'm pretty sure it's some kind of vegetable. Yummy.

"It's not edible."

Of course it is. I ate it, didn't I? Yes, I did. I ate some of the petals and one of the stems. And they were delicious. *Looks like a flower, tastes like a flower, it's a flower*, I tell them.

They keep untwining the flowers.

The boys aren't really helping. They're just talking about a video game. *Stop them already,* I call to them, but they don't even turn their heads.

Why won't anyone listen to me?

"We're done, Mrs. Cabbage," Maria says.

Really? They're done?

I hop forward to get a better look, but the girls are standing with their backs to me and I can't see the hat at all.

"Bring it here, girls," Mrs. Cabbage says.

The girls run to the front of the room where Mrs. Cabbage is.

I race to the other side of the cage, but I still can't see what they're holding.

Is it my hat?

The floor is covered in all the good stuff. Purple scarf, purple flowers, purple lace. Did they leave anything on the hat at all?

"This looks wonderful, girls," Mrs. Cabbage says. "T-Rab will love this. Shall we give it to him now?"

The girls nod.

They walk up to the cage. I'm so excited. I'm getting my hat back. My beautiful, wonderful nest-hat.

Mrs. Cabbage hands the girls an ugly brown *thing*.

It's not my hat. It can't be. It's not even purple anymore. It's just brown. And ugly.

All the purple stuff is on the floor. I want the purple

stuff!

I stamp my feet, but the girls just giggle.

"Go on and give it to him," Jonathan says. The boys have joined the girls at the front of the cage.

"I think we'll have to put it on the second floor, girls. There's really no room on the top floor, with his house and his litter box."

What kind of crazy talk is that? Ugly intruders aren't allowed in my palace anywhere. Don't these humans know anything?

Mrs. Cabbage opens the door to the second floor and the girls work on shoving that ugly thing into my palace. It takes them a while because even I can see the ugly thing is way too big for my palace. They end up folding it to fit it through the door, which is just wrong. If that were my purple nest, I'd be mad they folded it, but since it's just an ugly thing, I don't really care.

Except I don't want it in my palace at all.

I stamp my feet at them, but they just laugh. Why do they always do that?

I storm into my house and stamp again.

"Aw, don't you like your hat, T-Rab?" Derek asks.

That is not my hat, Mister, I tell him. *It's an ugly, brown thing and you can't make me play with it. I won't do it.*

Mrs. Cabbage tells them to make sure they clean up all my ribbon and flowers and lace. I stick my head out of my house and watch as the four children gather up all of my purple awesomeness.

What are they doing with it? Where are they taking it?

Mrs. Cabbage gives them a bag and they fill it to the brim.

I'm already planning what I'm going to do with that bag.

Mrs. Cabbage hangs it in the closet and announces, "I'll make you something beautiful to replace your hat, Ginger."

"Thanks, Mrs. Cabbage," Ginger says.

I wonder what she'll make. I wonder if it'll be as cool as my purple hat-nest.

Which reminds me.

An intruder has invaded my palace. It's just not right.

I hunker down to sulk.

The kids come back from recess and they get to work on a writing project. I stamp around on the top floor, mad about the intruder. Finally, I can't stand it anymore and I storm down the ramp.

What are you doing in here? I say to the ugly thing. *You're not supposed to be here. This is my palace. You need to leave.*

The thing doesn't move, so I kick my hind legs at it.

It doesn't do anything.

I try to walk around it, but it's too big. Why did they put this crazy, ugly thing in here, ruining my beautiful palace?

I want my purple hat-nest, I shout at Mrs. Cabbage. *I'm not happy with this impostor. You take him away and bring back my purple awesomeness.*

No answer.

I go up the ramp, but then I hop back down. *Fine, if you won't leave, I'll just eat you*, I say and I take a big bite out of its wide brim.

That was kind of yummy.

I take another bite.

It's like hay, only spicier. Yummy.

I contemplate the hugeness of this intruder and know that it'll take me weeks to eat it all. Weeks of this huge thing filling up my second floor, blocking the ramp to the first floor. *That is unacceptable,* I tell it.

It doesn't answer.

I grab it with my teeth and start to pull it up the ramp. I drag and drag, but it's so heavy and big, it's tough to move.

I make it halfway up, but then it gets stuck and we can't go anywhere. *You're too big,* I tell it. *I'll have to eat more of you.* I nibble at it forever, but it doesn't seem to get even a little bit smaller.

I hop to the top of the ramp, then turn and stare down at my ugly intruder. *Last warning,* I say. *Get out or I'm going to crush you.*

No answer.

I hop forward, take a flying leap and land on top of the intruder. I scratch hard at its surface and you'll never believe what happens.

Several long pieces of straw come out of it. It's like a scarecrow made of straw.

I scratch at it some more, then pick it up with my teeth and shake it.

Straw flies everywhere!

The humans are giggling, but I don't pay them any attention.

I'm too busy fighting my foe.

I warned you, I tell the intruder. *Now you're in trouble.* I rip more pieces of straw away, then toss the straw toward the wire walls. *Ha!* I crow in triumph. Several pieces of straw make it through the wires and land on the floor outside my palace. *You have been ejected!* I tell them and laugh my evil laugh.

The straw doesn't reply.

That's okay because I'm not done.

I work for ten thousand years tearing apart that ugly straw intruder until it's a pile of scraps that I can pull into my house and build into a nest.

When I'm finished, I collapse inside my house, surrounded by my straw-nest. It's not as colorful as my purple hat-nest, but it's still awesome since I'm the king of nest-makers.

"Bye, T-Rab."

I poke my head out of my house.

Ginger's standing at the door staring in at me.

I hop over to her.

She opens the cage and leans in.

I nudge her nose with mine.

She giggles. "See you tomorrow, T-Rab." She pets me, then closes and latches the palace door.

I stand on my hind legs and watch as she walks away.

Bye, Ginger, I say.

She waves her hand and disappears through the classroom door.

What are you looking at? I ask the tiger, who's staring at me again. *She's my human, not yours. Find your own classroom of humans. This one's mine.*

I hop into my house and curl up on my nest.

Tomorrow's going to be a fabulous day because my life is awesome. I live in a palace and I rule this territory with my powerful claws and fearsome teeth.

My name is Tyrabbisaurus Rex, but you can call me T-Rab, king of the classroom.

I want a bunny!

HAVING A BUNNY for a pet is a wonderful experience. However, caring for a rabbit is a very big responsibility and one that should be considered carefully. Do you have the time and the money to invest in years of caring for your faithful bunny companion?

Here are some things to consider before adopting a rabbit:

Space:

Bunnies need a lot of space. The cages sold in pet stores do not usually provide enough space for any bunny, even the miniature ones. Bunnies stand on their hinds legs to scope their surroundings. This is called telescoping. They should be able to do this in their cage. Therefore, the cage should be tall enough to allow the bunny to stand to his or her full height.

Bunnies will grow fast, so you need to consider the right cage for when they are an adult. Even if you have a cage that is big enough for your bunny to telescope, like T-Rab's cage, bunnies still need a lot of exercise. You should have an adequate amount of space for the bunnies to run and play.

If you are interested in T-Rab's cage environment,

his cage was modeled after a bunny condo created by Leith Petwerks (the real one is actually a LOT bigger!) You can visit their website at www.leithpetwerks.com

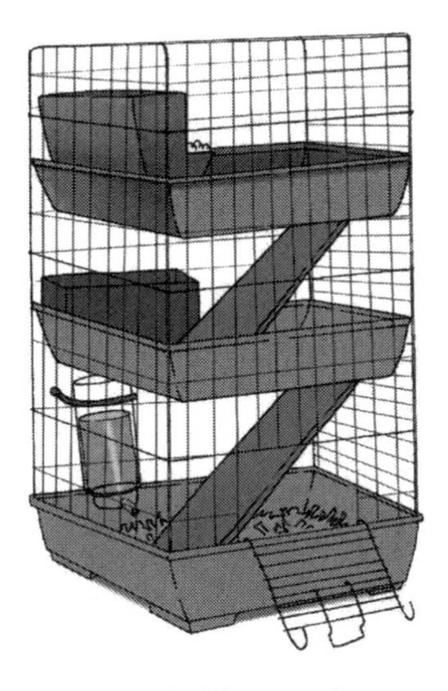

Bunnies hop very quickly and, as T-Rab did, will amaze you with their fast reflexes, ability to change direction mid-air and their absolute joy when given space for freedom of movement. Rabbits will scent-mark their territory by rubbing their chins against items they encounter on their route. This is their way of claiming objects and even people, and of finding their way to home base again (a burrow in the wild or in your home, their cage). If you've been rubbed by a bunny, they are saying that you belong to them!

Safety:

Bunnies will chew anything, as T-Rab has proven over and over again! This means that humans have to be very careful and bunny-proof any room a rabbit is in. All electrical cords should be hidden away from bunny eyes and teeth. Humans should be prepared for bunnies to mark anything in their path with their teeth. Bunnies have been known to chew rugs, books, furniture, curtains, peeling wallpaper, cords and pretty much anything they can get their teeth into. Be ready to examine your home from the ground up. What can your bunny see and get to and how can you make your bunny's environment safe for him or her?

Food:

As T-Rab has shown, bunnies love their food. They need a constant source of Timothy hay to help them digest their food properly. A bunny's hay feeder should never run empty. Bunnies also like their green vegetables every day. Some vegetables are very safe for bunnies and some should only be given in moderation. Some should never be given. You will need to spend some time researching what veggies are healthy for your bunny. Of course, bunnies can also be temperamental and quite emphatic about their tastes. A healthy veggie may be one a rabbit turns away (like T-Rab with his mustard greens) while a not-so-healthy vegetable a bunny may love, like carrots. Believe it or not, carrots are not good for bunnies because they are high in sugar and can cause tummy problems.

Finally, bunnies should be given some pellet food each day, to ensure they receive the proper nutrition. Seeds and nuts and many other ingredients found in rabbit food and treats are not healthy for bunnies. You will need to do your research to be sure you are giving your bunny healthy foods that will not harm him or her. Not all foods sold for rabbits are actually healthy for them to eat. Research to find the truth for yourself and for your bunny.

Water:

Bunnies, like all animals, need fresh water every day. You will need to make sure to provide this for them. Their water is usually given in a plastic water feeder. It is important to rinse this feeder out as part of your cleaning process.

A Clean Cage Environment:

Cages can become unhealthy very quickly. Your

bunny's cage environment, including the litter box, should be thoroughly cleaned at least once every week. It is also a good idea to do some spot cleaning every day. This will help make the weekly cleaning go faster. Any water spills should be cleaned immediately, as mold can grow quickly in a cage environment, which is unhealthy for bunnies and humans.

Playtime:

As we've seen with T-Rab, bunnies are very playful and have a lot of energy. They should be given time to play and exercise outside their cage every single day. Some wooden chew toys (like T-Rab's rattle) are safe for bunnies to play with unsupervised. Other toys bunnies should only play with while supervised. Pay careful attention to the tags on the toys before you remove them. Supervision is critical with curious, always-chewing-everything, enthusiastic bunnies.

Handle with Care:

T-Rab was very impressed that Mrs. Cavitch knew how to hold him. This is because bunnies are strong kickers and when frightened or unhappy may kick and struggle. If a handler is not trained in how to hold the rabbit properly, the bunny could manage to escape the handler's arms. Falls from any height can be very dangerous for bunnies. Children handling rabbits should be seated on the ground to ensure the safety of the bunny being held.

It's also important to know that bunnies aren't always cuddlers. It's not safe to sleep with a bunny at night and they may not ever enjoy being handled, cuddled or held for long periods of time. For a bunny, affection is given with the occasional chin rub, grooming behaviors like licking or gentle chewing and nudging with their nose or head. If you've received any of these gestures of affection from a bunny, it means you've been hugged bunny-style.

A Long-Term Commitment:

Bunnies can live to ten and even twelve years. *The Guiness Book of World Records* has reported the oldest rabbit in the world lived to age eighteen. This is fantastic news because it means your bunny companion can be with you for a decade or longer. However, it also means that adopting a bunny is a long-term commitment. Be certain you are willing and able to commit to many years of caring for your bunny companion.

Final Thoughts:

Clearly bunnies require a strong commitment to their care. There is a time and money investment in terms of providing the right cage environment, the proper nutrition and opportunities to play and exercise every day. The decision to adopt a bunny is not an easy one, but if you are willing to make this commitment, you may find your bunny has become your very best friend.

A.J. would like to thank...

- JEANINE HENNING, the very talented artist, who brought T-Rab to life with the cover art and illustrations in this book
- Allie, Josie, Kaitlynn & Megan, T-Rab's earliest readers and biggest fans
- Maria V. Snyder, who led many Writing Popular Fiction workshops at Seton Hill University, where early versions of *Tyrabbisaurus Rex* were critiqued
- Nikki Smith, who announced in one of those workshops, "I'm just going to call him T-Rab, if that's all right," thus giving Tyrabbisaurus Rex his most awesome nickname
- Carrie Gessner, Kathleen Kollman, Anna LaVoie, Annika Sundberg & Jenna Troughton for their constant encouragement and support
- Knuffle Bunny and Hunny Bunny, two Holland Lops who brightened my classroom year after year, bringing joy and companionship to countless students. Though they are no longer with us, they were the true inspiration behind T-Rab's character and his antics.

T-Rab would like to thank....

- MYSELF FOR being so awesome that I actually have my very own book
- The T-Rex council – NOT – for ignoring my plight as an imprisoned Tyrabbisaurus Rex
- Ginger for always wearing such tasty dresses and nest-worthy hats
- Maria for not being upset when I improved her puppy sweatshirt without her permission
- The tiger – NOT – for always staring at me with his beady little eyes
- Mrs. Cabbage for bringing me the yummiest of vegetables (except for when she tries to trick me with those impostor veggies – she gets NO thanks for those!)
- Scot and Amy at Leith Petwerks (www.leithpet werks.com) for building my prison palace (Mrs. Cabbage calls it a bunny condo). If I have to be locked up in a cage, it might as well have lots of space and toys and veggies in it, right?
- The vets and staff at Olathe Animal Hospital in Olathe, Kansas, for taking care of me when I'm sick (which is NEVER, people – I'm a fierce

tyrabbisaurus rex and we don't get sick!)

- The whiskered human and his loud *wroo-wroo-wroo-wroo* machine – NOT – for stealing my hay! I was saving that hay for later, mister. You bring it back soon or no thanks for you!
- Me for finally getting my story published! (I already thanked myself once, didn't I? Well, that's all right. I probably deserve more thanks than anybody. After all, I'm a Tyrabbisaurus Rex!)
- And YOU, ginormous human, for reading my story. Thank you!

Other books by A.J. Culey

CAN BE FOUND at www.ajculey.com

FOR EARLY READERS:

A Fairy's Job

If My Cat Could Fly

Salsa Visits the Zoo

Taco Runs Away

FOR YOUNG ADULT READERS:

Sehmah's Truth

The Trouble with Antlers

About the Author

A.J. CULEY IS a teacher, world traveler and writer. She lives with a number of very bossy cats and can be found at her website www.ajculey.com.

She can also be followed on Facebook at www.facebook.com/ajculey.author and on Twitter @ajculey.

T-Rab is also on Twitter @Tyrabbisaurus and can be found there when he manages to coax the laptop away from A.J.

About the Illustrator

PROFESSIONAL COVER DESIGNER and illustrator to authors and publishers worldwide, Jeanine's extensive 17 year professional background includes children's book illustration and publication, comic book art and publishing, book cover art, console game design and product branding.

She is however wondering where T-Rab took her pencils. And if in fact they still exist (she doubts it).

Made in the USA
San Bernardino, CA
13 December 2018